THE ADVENTURES

of

NATHANIEL B. OAKES

SECOND EDITION

NATHANIEL B. OAKES

Copyright © 2010 by Nathaniel B. Oakes

Published by J.D. Oakes Publishing, LLC

Second Edition

Spokane, WA
www.jdoakes.com

ISBN: 978-0-9844832-4-2

Printed in the United States of America

CONTENTS

To Mom and Dad,
Whose bountiful love nourished this sprightly brood,
And to my brothers and sisters
who sprouted so wondrously there from.

And especially many heart felt thanks
to my wife, Clarabelle,
who tends and mends me and the children.

On a cool August evening, I step down onto the running board of my pickup to unload my four children at my mother's house, and I am assailed with a symphony of thousands of crickets belting out their song. It is the crickets that capture my attention. Their love song quickly becomes mine. The sound of crickets always has this effect on me, this thrill of excitement, promise, and pleasure. It is a siren song, and I always follow— back to my first memory of life on the farm.

I was two and a half at the time. Sweet clover in full bloom stood three or four feet high all around. It practically engulfed our '55 Chevy station wagon parked in the middle of the field. No buildings stood on the forty-acre patch of slightly undulating prairie that snuggled up close to wooded hills.

A few of us kids tumbled in and out of the doors in play as Daddy and some of the older kids collected water from the old silica mine that shared a part of the western border of our soon-to-be farm. It was after dark, so we played by the light of the car's feeble dome light. The crickets sang loudly. And it was beautiful. It stuck indelibly in my young mind. Listen! The crickets are calling you, too. Don't resist. There are so many pleasurable tales waiting to be told. Soon, you will be cavorting around the farm with me. May you enjoy it now as I did then. A fair warning: watch out for the rooster.

Mom is alone now, but it wasn't always so. No, not alone at all. As it was, Alone couldn't have squeezed in anywhere. There wasn't room. Could it try to squeeze between Andy and Jake? No, Rose was right there. Could it try between Jeremy and Peter? Hardly. Nathaniel, Cecilia, and Ivan were there, already wedged rather tightly between the two. Surely a space could be found between Louisa and Marisa, but force as Alone might, it discovered Elizabeth, and Leo, both determinedly clutching onto their places. All right, let's go down the line and see if one of the littler ones was tiring and Alone could slip in unawares.

With a little effort and flying elbows, could a space be found between, Tristan and Jessica? Nope. Alone discovered Damien ensconced there, not budging.

So, the situation was that Mom never used to be alone. There were just too many children everywhere.

Oh, she and Alone found time together a little bit after everyone grew up, but we—that's my wife, Clarabelle, our four small children, and I—are chasing Alone away from the farm for a few hours so we can spend some time with Mom.

Now, if you were keeping count as we watched Alone trying to muscle his way into Mom's life, how many kids did you count? If you added up fifteen, you would be correct. Fifteen children all told. Really, that's all. No one else is hiding anywhere. Here's the lineup all in one breath: Louisa, Elizabeth, Leo, Marisa, Andy, Rose, Jake, Jeremy, Nathaniel, Cecilia, Ivan, Peter, Tristan, Damien, and Jessica.

No need to ask who was the most charming, dashing, smartest, and all-around fantastic child of this bunch. I will be gracious and offer the answer freely: I was. I applaud you for coming right to the source and asking me to avoid any confusion.

Now, that's a lot of little folks to digest, what with all those personalities just jumping off the page for you to meet. So let me ~ I'm Nathaniel ~ introduce them to you.

LOUISA

Louisa arrived first. I don't know why she got to be first. These things just happen, and we dealt with it. So there she was. Not bad, really. Well, actually pretty good. She was just a little more beautiful than Cleopatra and a bit smarter, too. Now, the great character historian Plutarch said that it wasn't so much Cleopatra's beauty that made her so charming, but that she could converse well with wit and eloquence that she commanded the greatest affection.

That's Louisa—beautiful and always talking. And she hated snakes. Of course, this combination of beauty and loathing of snakes afforded us little boys a veritable smorgasbord of opportunities to inflict delicious aggravation upon her.

"There's a snake!" Jeremy shouted as we walked through some tall grass.

"Where?" I asked excitedly.

"Right here," he replied, his hand clutching and grabbing at the matted grass trying to catch it. "It's a big bull snake."

This distinction was important. Bull snakes were pretty safe to grab and wouldn't generally bite. Not like the racer snakes. The racers were really hard to catch. They could slip and slither as if slathered with butter, and you had to be really quick to catch one. That was another thing about Louisa. She would protest when we got a snake too close to her by saying she didn't like those slimy things. Slimy?! We never met a single slimy snake, although the way racers could slither had Jeremy and me convinced that they must have been covered with snake oil.

I jumped to my hands and knees and spotted the snake as it slithered quickly to escape. I grabbed at the grass with my open hand and missed. Jeremy lunged and finally caught it. He held on tight as the bull snake tried to maintain its grasp of the matted grass it was partially beneath. Jeremy slowly rose from his knees as he extricated the snake from the tangles. "Must be close to three feet long," Jeremy said excitedly.

"Gosh, it's probably close to four," I replied as the snake tried to wind itself around his arm. "Let's go show Louisa!"

Showing Louisa snakes was always fun, but Louisa was not new to our desire to educate her on the ways of the snake. She had been our first student, and we regaled her with fresh knowledge all the time. She was a good sport and genuinely wanted to share in our enthusiasm for our coiled companions, but she had her limits.

We would usually approach her with whatever specimen we had corralled that day, and she would slowly back away and keep a safe distance. Her side of the conversation would usually go like this: "That's close enough ... What kind is it?... How do you know it doesn't bite?... No, I don't want to hold it ... No, no, that's close enough ... I don't want to feel the tongue lap my cheek ... No, no, that's all right ... Yes, I do think it's pretty ... Yes, it does have neat trimmings ... No, I don't want to pet it ... I don't like touching slimy things ... Yes, yes, that's close enough ... Yes, I know, but how do you know this one doesn't bite? ... Yes, I do think it's neat how you guys catch them, but no, don't you dare let it go right here."

One day, the family encountered a snake that will never forget Louisa. The unforgettable encounter happened one summer evening as Louisa returned from town in her 1968 Mercury. Our forty-acre farm was quite a ways from the county road we lived on, so we had a thirty-foot-wide driveway a quarter of a mile long stretching from our house to the road. As she rumbled up the drive, lost in some reverie or another, she suddenly realized that she was about to roll over a massive snake. At first she thought it was a small log that had fallen across the road. It was stretched across the driveway, warming itself in the summer sun. It was too late to even touch the breaks. Thump went the front wheels; then thump went the rear wheels.

As shock and dismay shook Louisa, she hit the accelerator and the Mercury flew as fast as the god it was named for. She was doing nearly forty when she hit our property line and was edging toward sixty when she passed baby Jessica digging holes with her spoon at the entrance of the yard. Louisa stomped on the brake and, in a hail of gravel and dust, skidded to a stop. She leapt out of the car and shouted to us boys, Jeremy, Jake and me, about the humongous snake she had just run over. It only took a second for Jeremy to begin sprinting up the driveway to look at the gigantic snake Louisa was trying to describe in a frenzy of excitement. Jake, still recovering from the shock of Louisa's cacophonous entrance, picked up his wits and hightailed it after Jeremy. Dad, fearing it might be a rattler, ran to the shed for a shovel and then followed in hot pursuit.

Jeremy was the first to arrive and see the serpent. And indeed, it did look like everything the word serpent inspired. It had a huge, thick, diamond-shaped head with a bulging jaw. Its black eyes looked malevolent under their hoods. The incredibly thick body made

Jeremy's arm look like a spaghetti stick. Jeremy had caught many snakes, but he could not will himself to grab this one. As Jeremy watched incredulously, Jake arrived just in time to watch the snake crawl into a squirrel hole at the base of a small haystack near the side of the road. Dad arrived too late to see it. Jeremy and Jake didn't see any rattles on it, but Dad tore the haystack apart anyway to make sure it was no danger to the children. But the snake was never to be seen again—although it told stories.

Bull snake families scattered across our forty acres have heard it said that their grandfather was nearly killed by the god Mercury. The serpent patriarch would describe dozing off in delicious solitude on a bucolic country lane, when, suddenly, Mercury, driven by Cleopatra, bore down upon him with malicious intent and rolled over him with a four-wheeled chariot. After being thus indignantly trod upon, he was attacked by two savages (Jeremy and Jake) and a large, fully clothed armed warrior (Dad), whose death-dealing weapon he barely managed to escape. Of his ninety-two vertebra, four in his neck and five in his lower back were broken . . .

Now, I don't know if I can quite believe this. Just where does a snake's neck end and his lower back begin? Isn't a snake all neck?

Anyway, we'll let him tell his story.

ELIZABETH

Elizabeth made her grand appearance fifteen months after Louisa was born. Now, mind you, I didn't know her name was Elizabeth until I was about nineteen. I always thought her name was Gut. Yeah, it's a nice name for a pretty girl, don't you think? Louisa was the one who managed to give this name to Elizabeth. In high school, Louisa and Elizabeth both took Spanish as a second language. Elizabeth called Louisa Juanita, and Louisa called Elizabeth Cutalina. Cutalina, spoken gutturally, sounds a lot like Gutalina, and when this is shortened, of course, you get Gut. Now, whether Louisa had a habit of speaking gutturally, I can only surmise. But, now that I think of it, that might explain why many of her 402 boyfriends looked like Neanderthals, back when hair was in and grunts were considered intelligent. Anyway, Gut it was.

Despite her name, Elizabeth was very caring. She cared deeply. She was our carer-in-residence. She even cared for snakes; for years, she slept with a fourteen-foot purple snake that she got for her birthday. But nothing showed her care more than the time Dad installed new electrical wire in our house.

"Now listen closely as I explain what might happen and what I want you kids to do," Dad said as he tied a piece of rope around one wrist and then one to the other wrist. Elizabeth listened with complete attention and had already begun to worry. She could smell the possibility of danger and feared the worst. Louisa listened closely and took it all in stride. "We'll deal with it when it happens" was her motto. Leo, always the big brother and someone who could understand anything mechanical, was eager to hear what he could to do to help Dad.

"See these wires?" Dad asked as he pointed into the electrical box. "These wires have electricity in them, which is very dangerous to touch. Usually you only get a shock, but sometimes there's so much electricity in them that it can kill you."

Worry was running laps around the inside of Elizabeth's stomach.

"These big wires here, you see, are filled with so much electricity that if I touch or hold them wrong, my hand won't be able to let go and I'll be stuck. I want you kids to pull on these ropes to pull my hand off the wires if that happens." This seemed perfectly reasonable to Louisa. She wasn't worried because she knew Dad wouldn't be doing the job if there was any chance of a mishap. To Leo, this was an adventure, and he was eagerly waiting to begin. Marisa, at her age, couldn't fathom real danger, so she thought it might be fun to see it happen. Andy continued to play with his army men. But Elizabeth did what came naturally—she worried. A lot. She worried for all of the family. In fact, everyone else lent their worries to her so that they could all race around together in Elizabeth's stomach.

As Dad turned and faced the electrical panel, ten huge eyes in five little heads concentrated on his hands. He reached for the wire. Louisa and Elizabeth lined up by the right rope, ready to pull Dad off the wire if he froze to it; Leo, Marisa, and Andy were on the left. Dad grasped the wire with his left hand. All the worries that had been racing around in Elizabeth tried to leap up from her stomach at the same moment. Quickly, she gulped hard, closing the means of escape.

Dad reached for the other wire, and again Elizabeth's worries scrambled wildly, pushing each other and clawing their way up her throat. This battle raged nonstop as Dad continued his work. The contents of her stomach traveled continuously up and down until Dad finished the job, which never seemed to end.

When he was finished, as each of the other kids went coolly about their business, Elizabeth slithered away to a quiet corner of the unfinished house, tired, exhausted, and limp, to recompose her innards until her next adventure of worry. She was nine years old and still had a long way to go, for her cheery disposition and her empathy for others stayed with her on the long way to womanhood. As she was a natural nurse, we all benefited from her self-sacrifice on our long ways to life on our own.

LEO

Leo entered the light of this world as the oldest brother. I don't see why he got to be the oldest brother just because he came first. But what was a little brother to do?

Fortunately, Leo was well-equipped for his august position. On rare occasions, we little brothers were allowed a glimpse of the mystery of how he earned his title of big brother. Peering into the top drawer of his dresser, we were able to see all the tools of his craft: boxes of ammunition, arrowheads and nocks, bow strings, old Indian-head nickels, silver dollars, self-crafted leather sheaths, and knives. However, we were only allowed a glimpse into this world if Leo himself was showing us through it.

And so it was one fine evening when we were peering into the drawer, Leo allowed us to look back to the very beginning of his adventure as big brother. He carefully dug past all his items and gingerly lifted out an old cigar box. The box was, to say the least, really, really neat. It was at least four hundred years old. It was wooden and had King Edward's picture right on it, with him sitting kingly on his throne in red robes with gold lions surrounding him. The box had real gold hinges and a beautiful working latch. In the box, Leo kept five things: the pair of boxing gloves he was born wearing, the two tools the little men used to remove his tonsils, and a worn stuffed monkey that accompanied him on his earliest journey of being a big brother. I guess even big brothers needed help sometimes. That is hard to imagine, really, with big brothers being who they are, and Leo was the biggest. He knew everything. But, there was the monkey to prove that even Leo had needed help starting out. It was very bedraggled and must have worked very hard at being Leo's companion.

As I mentioned, there were tonsil-removing tools along with the boxing gloves and monkey. These, a pickax and shovel, were left behind by the little men who had removed Leo's tonsils.

Because I was not present when Leo had his operation, I can only depend on his first-hand account and the physical evidence for verification. The pickax and shovel were indeed small, Leo did not have his tonsils, and having only been sedated when the men went to work, he was fully aware of all the particulars of his operation. What's more, he was a full four years old at the time. Memory is always crystal clear at that age, and you could make a sure bet that nothing but the truth was being told as Leo related his story.

"The doctors laid me flat on my back and told me to open my mouth as far as I could so the little men would have no trouble driving their dump trucks in and out. But first I had to get a shot (which didn't hurt at all) that would keep me from talking to the men, as they were very shy and might be scared away before they finished me off or finished the job, whichever came first. Well, I opened my mouth very wide when they poked that needle in my fanny. I was hoping to let them know of my displeasure with the loudest of hollers, hence the wide-open mouth, but before I could even commence the first note of complaint, I heard the doctor boom, 'Count down from ten to zero out loud '

"Well, I managed ten and nine, but I don't remember getting to eight. All I know is the miners started moving in. They came in marching—some with pickaxes, some with shovels, some with wheelbarrows, and some with hoes. They marched right up my pillow, climbed up my chin, conquered my lip, and slid right down my tongue and into my throat. Before them rose a mountain of tonsil, which they had one hour to remove. They jumped right in to work. They dug with the picks and shoveled with the shovels. They hauled with the barrows and hoed with the hoes. The wheelbarrow, heaped high with tonsil ore, was wheeled up my throat, hauled over my tongue, hooked onto block and tackle (no, not the football kind), run up to my lips, and pitched down my chin into the dump trucks waiting below.

"Mom always said she thought we had just a tidbit of Irish in us. Well, those tiny little leprechauns dug so deep that any Irish I might have had was thrown out with the blarney. At least I think they got all the blarney. Sure hope so. Not healthy "

We nodded our heads in agreement; we didn't want our big brother to have any blarney left in him, it being mixed up in that tonsil ore and all.

With a wave of his hand, he finished up with, "And that's how I got these little tools. When the doctor hollered, 'All's well that hurts like 'ell,' two of the little guys who had been twanging the stalactite hanging down from the top of my throat, instead of working, carelessly left their tools behind. The little people shot out of my mouth and into thin air, never to be heard of again."

And as for the boxing gloves, all I know is that he was born with them. At least, that's what Leo said, and he should know—he was there. But, strangely, having been born seven years later, I barely remember the particulars of that event.

MARISA

Marisa arrived just ahead of Andy. Andy was the fifth, so that made Marisa the fourth. Not Marisa the IV. Just Marisa the fourth of the fifteen. She came tripping into this life. I am not sure she was really born *per se*. She just tripped, and *voila*, there was Marisa. She wasn't really clumsy; she was just happy and busy like lots of little girls. She never knew where she was going, and so her feet didn't either. They just tried hard to stay underneath her and do what they were made to do: walk, run, skip, and trip. This caused our Dad a bit of exasperation.

Dad would pull to a stop in front of school in our 1965 four-wheel-drive International Travelall and turn around to watch the kids as they unloaded from the car. Louisa was out, standing, now walking—good. Elizabeth was out, upright, and walking—good. Leo was out, also upright—good. Marisa—whoosh! Her head would disappear below the door. Dad would scramble out of his door and run around the car to find Marisa flat on her back, halfway under the car with one hand clutching her lunchbox and the other hand holding her book bag. Her feet would be flailing around as she tried to right herself. "Now, I told you to pay attention and watch where you're stepping so you don't fall down," he would say with exasperation.

If there was any patch of ice within forty-two miles of her, even if it was the size of a postage stamp, Marisa's feet would find it. When her feet would find the ice, they wouldn't tell her. They'd just slip on it and let her figure out an explanation to tell Dad. However, Marisa's feet didn't need ice to cause her trouble.

So the next time, Daddy would pull up to the curb and the others would disembark without incident. Marisa, never one to disappoint—whoosh! Down she would go. Now, she knew there was no ice. She had gotten her feet to stop arguing about who belonged on the right and who on the left and had tried with every effort to get out of the car like a normal person—upright, not prostrate. No such luck. But how was she supposed to know that her left leg had decided to go to sleep on the long drive to school? Her right leg stood up like any upstanding leg ought to, but when her left leg was asked to do the same, it failed, and down she went.

Marisa always found a way to get on her feet again. It stands her in good stead as she adventures along. She stands tall to this day!

ANDY

Andy was born in a dessert. It was very hot in the dessert. I remember when Mom would take a dessert from the oven she would tell us not to touch it. It was just too hot. Now, how a person could be born in a dessert, I don't know, but Andy said he was. And I don't remember it as well as he—I wasn't born yet.

The name of the dessert was Phoenix and it was in a foreign country called Arizona. It was just too hot for Dad and Mom. It was so hot all the time that Dad lost all of his appetite and could only drink milk. Now, I think milk and dessert go extremely well together, but the doctor told Dad that if he was only going to drink milk in the dessert all the time, he had better move to another part of the country. It's a real bear to lose your health in a dessert; it's better to just move to the farmland.

Andy was the best archer among us. One fine early

spring afternoon, Leo, Jeremy, Ivan, Peter, and myself were whiling away the afternoon by sitting, lounging, and slouching on the rails of the pigpens when suddenly Jeremy said, "Let's watch Andy shoot."

Andy was in the field next to ours, which had been abandoned years before and now played host to various varmints and other wildlife. In particular, two colonies of ground squirrels made their home in that field. One colony was just fifty yards off our northern property line. The other colony was a good two hundred yards farther. Andy was at the closer one, stalking a squirrel that had already spotted him.

We would shoot at these critters from anywhere from five to thirty yards away—with archery, the closer the better. Now, these squirrels were no slouches. They were country-born and country-bred: wary, smart, and fast. They could see an arrow coming, thumb their noses at it, and dodge it with ease. Part of a hunter's skill was in deciding whether to shoot at a squirrel directly or to anticipate where it was going to run and hit it in flight.

These squirrels were laying it all on the line, daring Andy to best them. But Andy was in top form. He was slightly bent over, his 45# Bear recurve bow skillfully held in his half-bent left arm and three fingers on his right hand holding the knocked arrow on the string. He ever so slowly raised his left foot and, with painstakingly slow motion, moved it through the air, placing it softly on the ground. He repeated this motion with his right foot. Continuing this achingly slow motion forward, he hoped to get within shooting range.

The squirrel was at its haughtiest, standing straight up on a mound of dirt. With its burrow hole directly below it, the squirrel chirruped a taunt at Andy. Andy inched forward. At about ten yards, he stopped. He slowly raised his bow arm and imperceptibly straightened his body. When he was almost upright and had his bow arm extended, he began to ever-so-slightly draw the string back. His eye took in every twitch of the squirrel to see if its nerve would break and cause it to dive for its hole. Every split-second he was deciding whether to shoot at it or at the hole.

We all sat perfectly still, watching this drama play out. Could Andy pull this off with a crowd watching? Would the squirrel lose its nerve and dive for cover?

Andy pulled back on the string and had only a few more inches of his thirty-inch draw to go. His fingers touched his chin and he released the shaft. It flew true. We couldn't believe it. The squirrel was struck from its perch. Andy ran up to his kill, bent over to retrieve his arrow, and—what do you know?—another squirrel popped up about twenty yards farther away and dared Andy to do it again. We doubled that dare. We were all squirrel hunters and knew how hard it would be to knock off two saucy squirrels in a row.

Andy heard the second squirrel chirp at him, so he slowly raised his head from his bent-over position. He spotted the squirrel a good twenty yards out from him. Again, Andy had to decide if he should try to knock the squirrel from its perch or catch it on the dive.

Andy painstakingly straightened, smoothly knocked another arrow, and repeated the slow draw. With his eye never leaving the jaunty squirrel, he once again let the shaft fly. And again he shot true.

Talking excitedly, we ran across the field to Andy and congratulated him on his victory. That was Andy, always steady and excellent at whatever he did. We allowed the squirrel to tell its side of the story from its future spot on the wall.

ROSE

Rose was our birthday-cake baker, cookie cutter, pie maker, and seamstress. Let me tell you about her adventure with the gooseberry pie.

One day, Dad was talked into bringing home a sprig of a gooseberry bush from a guy at work. His co-worker promised that the bushes needed little care, even less water, and would grow profusely. Boy, was he right. The bush took to growing like there was no tomorrow, which is a good thing because a tomorrow is iffy for a gooseberry bush once its fruit has been tasted.

The bush grew right near a telephone pole—at least that's what we called the pole. It was really an electrical pole, but we called all poles like it a telephone pole. Anyway, on a fine fall day, the bush was full of fruit and was ripe for the plucking. So pluck them Rose did. She got a full bowl of ripe gooseberries. Then she took them to the kitchen to work her magic.

Her first problem was to decide whether to remove the stems or not. She figured the stems were so tiny, what would be the harm in leaving them on? So she rinsed the berries and commenced with adding the sugar and all the other things you do to make a pie.

After the pie was fresh out of the oven, she opened the back door and called us in: "Come and get it!"

We didn't need to be told what "it" was; dessert was a little rare those days, so when there was any hint of it hanging around, we hung around, too. We all rushed to the door and into the house and pulled up our chairs in anticipation of a nice big slice of this new kind of pie. And Rose was generous, too; we all got a nice, big piece. After saying grace, we plunged our spoons into the steaming mass of reddish, stemmy mush. Then the spoons traveled to our mouths, all at a pretty even pace, and then past our lips and onto our tongues.

There, it was met with absolute rejection. Absolute and utter rejection. Our tongues were shocked and recoiled in horror. Our eyes flew open in stark surprise. We tried to give it a swish around the mouth to give it a fair shake, but we couldn't do it. With no uncertainty, the mush reversed its course. It moved off the tongue, out the lips, and onto the plate even faster than it had gone in. It was the most revolting concoction ever devised by man or woman. Rose concocted it, and we rejected it. We had to grab our throats and squeeze to keep the rest of the contents of our stomach down, all of which seemed to want to come up and see what all the excitement was about.

Just before we were able to say how awful it was (without hurting Rose's feelings, of course), she daintily tried a lick herself and immediately blanched. With that, we were all able to start exclaiming how awful the pie was, and we all began to laugh. Including Rose. She laughed until she cried.

Rose took the pie outside and set it in the backyard. The dog ran up eagerly to see what tasty dish was set before him, but his enthusiasm began to wane as he approached and could see what the mound of food looked like. He slowed to a slink, crawled up to the plate, stretched out his nose with an exploratory sniff, and then shrank back in disgust. He looked up at us with an expression of disdain, as if to say, "You expect me to eat that? I'm a respectable dog, you know. Do I look like a buzzard?" He then skulked away, insulted.

After the dog abandoned the dish, my pet magpie, Marvin, swooped down to espy what all the commotion was about. He saw the pie, and it seemed good to him. Eating anything rotten, old, and dead was what God had made him for, but he preferred fresh and juicy.

And the pie was fresh, juicy, and soft, so without a moment's hesitation, he landed on the edge of the pie dish and plunged his beak in all the way. Yikes! He tried to jerk his beak out, but the mess stuck and pulled him back in, as if trying to swallow him up. He rocked back and forth and shook with gusto, and the mess eventually let go. But you have never seen such frantic antics that that bird went through to expel the mess from his beak. His tongue worked rapidly, trying to push it out of his mouth. He swiped his beak back and forth on the ground in a frantic attempt to get it out. He ruffled his feathers in indignation, flew off to nurse his hurt feelings and washed the whole sorry incident away in a delicious mud puddle.

JAKE

Jake arrived before Jeremy and me. It wasn't so much that he had broader shoulders or was stronger; no, it was because there were cute nurses ready to greet him. And greet him they did. He just came out and winked at them, and they were smitten. "Oh, he's so cute" and "how precious" and "he's so handsome," they said as they fought over him, trying to decide who was to weigh, bathe, and swaddle him. He just winked a few more times and swam pleasantly in a sea of attention.

That was Jake. All the girls liked him. Yes, I said all. That didn't leave any to spill over for Jeremy and me. You think I'm exaggerating? Okay, so how about the time two of the neighbor girls rode their horses over. We'd never seen them before. None of us had. Then there was Jake, just cool as a cucumber, carrying on and jawing away as if he'd known them forever. The girls, sitting up on their horses, flirted and carried on with him as if Jeremy and I didn't even exist. And oh, how sickening to see him give them that wink as they turned to go, the girls giggling and practically melting off their horses.

Or how about the time, the neighbors' little blond cousin came down to see us? Yep, there was Jake. Even before Jeremy and I had lifted our jaws off the ground, Jake was bringing her over to the pigpens to show her our pigs. Now, I ask, what blond city-girl is going to go gaga over pigs? Well, that one did. And all because of that wink. Jeremy and I together were at least half as strong as Jake, which must have been pretty impressive, but girls just passed right on by us as if we weren't even there.

We seldom had strangers as company at our farm, and when we did, it usually was someone inquiring about the silica quarry that bordered the west side of our property. One hot, lazy summer afternoon, we were all lollygagging around the house, teasing each other and making a nuisance of ourselves, when we heard the sound of a car motor in the yard and our dog barking. We all made a mad dash to the windows to see what was up. Wow—there were girls spilling out all over the yard. Blonds, brunettes, ebonites, redheads, and I don't know what else.

The dog was of no use. Where under usual circumstances he would bellow his disapproval of visitors in a deep, controlled, well-modulated, masculine voice, here he was so discombobulated by the sea of femininity that he totally lost his mind. Jumping around in a most undignified fashion, he squeaked out the most embarrassing falsetto of barks. Any pretense to being a great defender of life and property melted away. He wasn't going to be any help in finding out who these *femmes fatales* were. He invited them into the house to let Mom figure it out.

Jeremy wasn't going to be any help, either. His larynx was jammed up with his tongue, and he was also speaking in an embarrassing falsetto, so we couldn't let him out of the house. Me? All coolness I kept my wits. I kept them so close, I couldn't speak. Somewhat like a dimwit, only handsomer. Since we were all rendered useless by the sudden apparition of beauty that came out of nowhere, it fell to Mom to go out and invite them in. So she did.

Jeremy and I disappeared outside, as if the onslaught of femininity held absolutely no interest for us. Mom held a polite conversation about nothing with them. They kept looking around as if expecting something, and when it was clear that the something was not to be, they politely got up and left. It was only later that we found out that Jake had winked at one of them on his way to work and that *that* one had told her gaggle of friends. Then they had all come down to see if they could get a glimpse of him.

We never saw them again.

JEREMY

I was still preparing for my turn to come into the world in a year so I never actually saw Jeremy arrive.

Have you ever seen a bunch of children trying to catch a frantic frog? The kids jump, lunge, and grab, getting all tangled up as the frog leaps erratically across the ground to elude the mob. Well, that's what I hear it was like for the nurses when Jeremy somersaulted into the world. He was the athlete.

Jeremy came out with a cartwheel, catapulted

himself onto the scale, slid across the changing table, performed a swan dive into the bath, snapped a nurse with a towel, caught the bar of soap with one hand as it shot from her hand in surprised indignation, slam dunked it into the sink, did a handstand on the parallel bars of the hospital bed, and dove into a pile of blankets where he was quickly swaddled and trundled off to the nursery. It was all downhill from there.

Jeremy's athleticism was a very good thing. For him, of course, but for me especially. Jeremy was one of those guys that could make anybody else on his team look good. In football, if I was quarterbacking, it would look like this: I drop back for a pass play, look up for a receiver, see 160 pounds of defensive back bearing down on me from the right and look to the left to see a 150-pound freight train hurtling towards me. Terror grips me around the chest, and I hurl the ball downfield in a desperate attempt to save my life. The action stops around me as all look downfield to see what kind of melee the desperately and wildly thrown ball is going to cause, when, out of nowhere, there is Jeremy sailing effortlessly on winged shoes to make a picture-perfect catch. Applause and congratulations all around: "Wow what a beautiful throw! How did you manage to time that throw so perfectly that only Jeremy was able to get it amid all those defenders?"

Or, if I were to block for Jeremy: There's Jeremy, ball in hand, screaming downfield around the left side of the defense. There's me, blocking to the right. Stop. Rewind. There's me squashed flat, a size ten cleat print neatly imbedded in chest. I raise my face from six inches below the turf to see Jeremy neatly sidestep the defender that just mowed me down and glide on downfield to glory. Then teammates are piling on top of me, pounding and slapping me on the back: "Man, what a block!" And why did I get this credit? Because when Jeremy would say "nice block" or "nice throw," all the teammates would believe him. As well they should—he had just made the play.

But I always knew Jeremy was the only reason I looked good. Whenever I was in trouble, I would just yell, "Jeremy," and hurl the ball in his direction, and unfailingly, Jeremy would make the play.

So in sports, so in life.

CECILIA

Why Cecilia came, I'm not sure. She did, though. She just strolled out after me, as pretty as a cucumber and a bit cleverer. You would have thought that divine providence would have stopped at me. How one could think otherwise, I don't know. Did God really think we needed a number ten? I was sort of like the delicious cream that rose to the top, the bloom on the rose, the cherry on the chocolate sundae, so why the need for Cecilia?

Wait! No need to start piling on all the reasons. I know someone will mention how witty she was, like when I would flex my Atlas-like body and say with so much nonchalance to Cecilia, "Look at my muscles," and she would begin to hurriedly look under the cushions of the couch, under the tablecloth, in her back pocket, and anywhere but at me. Very funny! Or someone will mention how quiet and unassuming she was.

Now anybody can afford to be quiet when she does her nefarious dealings while asleep. Cecilia and I slept across from each other for the better part of our childhood. When we were little, to accommodate the overflow of kids in the sleeping area of our house (what we called "back by the beds"), Cecilia slept on the living room couch and I slept on a cot next to her, which I assembled every night and then took down and stored back by the beds during the day. Later, when some of the others kids had grown up and moved out, we inherited the bottoms of two of the bunk beds that were across from each other. Countless times, Cecilia would be fast asleep and then begin to sleepwalk, and in this state she would steal my blankets, my pillow, and sometimes the pajamas off my back.

Yes, I would be slumbering peacefully in my own field of dreams, effortlessly shooting the eyetooth out of a tiger with my slingshot, when suddenly a violent shake of my bed would snap me awake. I would see Cecilia stretched full-length from her bed to my pillow, trying to jerk it out from under my head. Now, having my head treated roughly and my pillow plucked, pulled, and pilloried in the middle of the night did not prepare me for the most intelligent of conversations, but it did allow for some fun. Usually the conversations went like this:

Me: Cecilia, what are you doing?

Cecilia: I want my pillow.

Me: You have your pillow.

Cecilia (shaking me vigorously): This is *my* pillow!

Me: No, *your* pillow is right under you.

Then she would insist again that it was her pillow and try again to maneuver it from me. Then I would catch on that she was asleep, and I would say, "You're asleep, so just go to sleep." (Isn't it intelligent to tell some one who is asleep to go to sleep?)

Cecilia: I'm not asleep, so just give me my pillow.

Me: You are asleep, and you're not going to remember any of this in the morning.

Cecilia: I am not asleep, and I *will* remember this in the morning. [Here she would start to cry.]

Me: Okay, then I'm asking you right now if you're going to remember this tomorrow morning.

And she would insist that she would. I would even make her promise. By that time, her crying and my talking to her would wake Mom, and she would come in and ask what the matter was. I would have to tell her that Cecilia was asleep and trying to take my pillow. It would take Mom telling Cecilia to give it back to me to make Cecilia surrender her grasp on my pillow. Sure enough, the next day I would ask her if she remembered the attempted purloining the night before, and she would categorically deny all of the previous night's events.

In contrast to my appearance in pictures of me,

I am quite sure I was born with straight hair, but after all the times I was wrenched, cajoled, shaken, upended, thrown, and subjected to every other form of harassment Cecilia could inflict, my hair now stands in a perpetual state of shock. Yes, Cecilia—that quiet, cute, and witty girl—followed me out into the world. And I'm glad she did!

IVAN

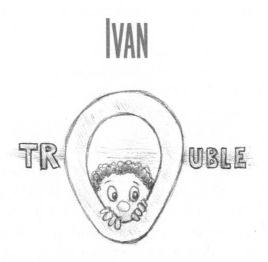

TR⬭UBLE

"No one comes to me unless the Father calls him." So says the Good Book. Now Ivan might have launched his career upon the stage of life before me, if he and I hadn't often heard our names wrong. I might have had to follow Cecilia out into the world. Or it might have been Ivan who had heard wrongly when Father called us forth from the womb. Maybe he had thundered, "Ivan," and I, thinking He had said, "Nathaniel," left off my diving lessons (there was just so much time for swimming in there), and hurriedly slipped from my swimming trunks into my birthday suit and presented myself in shining splendor to the world, beating Ivan to it.

You see, when people—especially Dad—would call for Ivan or me, there were usually many mix-ups. These mix-ups took place because the names Nathaniel and Ivan often sounded the same, particularly when said loudly and from a distance. "How is *that*?" you ask. Well, I can't tell you because I don't know. They aren't phonetically the same and they don't rhyme, so there doesn't seem to be a valid reason why.

"Nathaniel!" I heard Dad calling urgently, but from far off in the distance.

I was a ways up the old road that led up into the silica mine by our farm. Crouched down and leaning forward as far as I could, I held out a juicy strawberry trying to lure a wild chipmunk into eating it from my hand. I had been in this position for about half an hour, and our patience—mine and the chipmunk's—was wearing thin. Mine because I was getting mighty uncomfortable and the chipmunk's because his passion for the juicy strawberry was enticing him beyond his means of resistance. So, although I was in a mental tug-of-war with the chipmunk, Dad's summons impelled me to leave off the serene pastime and hightail it home.

I leapt a goodly six feet in the air from my crouched position and started running six or seven steps in the air before I even landed on the ground and tore off to home. I leapt, sailed, glided, and soared over rocks, stumps, streams, and stones. I swerved, turned, skidded, and bounced off trees, boulders, bears, and burrows. I careened around, crashed through, and mowed over, brush, briars, and the occasional bramble. I catapulted over a fence and shot out of the woods into the yard. And there was Dad, leisurely repairing another fence—and Ivan nonchalantly harassing the dog. Panting, I waited for my breath to catch up—as it was still tangled up in a barbed wire fence a few hundred feet behind me. I walked up to Dad with what composure I had left and asked him what he wanted. He looked up at my harried face with a surprised smile. Now, fancy that! Once again, my plans were foiled by mis-hearing my name. It turned out that he had actually called Ivan, and it had only *sounded* like Nathaniel from a distance.

This is the way that Ivan inadvertently interrupted my otherwise tranquil life. The *vertent* ways were legion—because no matter what trouble I got into, Ivan was always there. Now, I don't mean "Trouble" with a big "T," just "trouble" with a small "T." This trouble is what followed Ivan around, and somehow my troubles always seemed to be tangled up with Ivan's. Now, a dispassionate observer might think I got into trouble on my own or that I led Ivan into trouble, but that's the problem with dispassionate observers—they tend to be dispassionate. In that unnatural state, they start making judgments in Ivan's favor, and where does that leave *me*? The trouble Ivan and I got into must wait for its own section in the tales that follow (as we did, in fact, follow each other around), and we had an equal share of adventure and misadventure. In either case, it was always delightful to have him around.

PETER

I am not certain, even after these long years, whether Peter was actually born and if it happened the way he said. I'm not certain whether it was really where he says it was or if it happened in another place. I never thought to ask Mom. I don't think it would have been of much consequence to her how it actually happened. With so many storks flying in over the years, each baby started to look pretty much like any other. But Peter arrived, and that's the important thing.

Peter was a master storyteller, and the taller the story, the better. He was the tallest-tale teller to take to telling a tall tale as ever was told. (No, he wasn't the tallest tale-teller; you got mixed up. He was smaller; I was taller; and I could tell a fair- to middling-height tale myself. He was *smaller*, not taller, but he could still tell a taller tale.)

To watch him, even when he was as young as six or seven, start into a tale at a slow crawl, gather steam, expand the adjectives, blow more and more hot air into it, pick up speed, discard all fact or reason until all was pure fancy, and then let it float out was a beautiful thing. We had a terrific time trying with might and main to poke holes in his creations, but by the time he had let go of it, it had solidified in his mind that it was the truth. There was no budging him out of it. Not by one of us kids anyway.

There was only one thing that could butt Peter enough to make him budge, and that was a battering ram. Not the kind that the medieval warriors used to storm castle doors. No, the real thing that gave those battering rams their name.

Many were the bovine, feathered, cloven-hoofed and furry animals that graced the farm throughout our childhood years, and sheep were numbered among them. McCoy stars here. He was the real thing. A male sheep all grown up.

Now when McCoy was born it was Peter's job, along with Tristan and Damien, to tend the sheep. These three shepherds thought that tending would be a lot more interesting if teasing could be introduced into the care of the flock, and so they did. The introduction seemed a good idea almost immediately as lambs are particularly frolick as kids, these even more than most, as kids are baby goats and these lambs took umbrage

THE ADVENTURES OF NATHANIEL B. OAKES

at storytellers who don't know the difference between a lamb and a kid.

Now Peter was the first to discover that lambs love to butt heads as they prance about and play with one another. Peter would drop down on his hands and knees and raise one hand up to the height of the lamb's head and let one charge with all its infantile might into his hand. This delighted Peter and the lambs. Now McCoy took to this game with even more gusto than the rest and became Peter's special sparring partner. As a little time went by, Peter made his hand into a fist so that McCoy could whack into a more solid object, like another lamb's head. As time went on, and McCoy got bigger, Peter had to start using both hands. Shortly, he had to stand up, and soon he had to stand up with both hands braced against his bent knees to withstand the impact of McCoy's charge. Well this little game was all fine and dandy when the lamb was little. But little boy lambs grow up to be big bad rams and McCoy was no exception.

One fine day, we boys spilled into the pasture that served as our football field and the sheep's sustenance. Unbeknownst to us, McCoy was listening as we boys talked of flying tackles, teeth shattering blocks and the advantage of surprise. He was especially interested in the advantage of surprise and put it to the test right away.

As Peter was holding the football and expostulating loudly about the absolute necessity of not budging from one's place as one accepted a block or a charge from an opponent, McCoy planned his move. He waited. Peter looked to his left, then to his right. McCoy never took his eye off his target. Peter bent down to demonstrate the proper stance for a football line man. McCoy saw his chance. His hoofs clove the soil as they bit in for traction. Topsoil flew in clods as McCoy launched his attack on Peter's rear. Peter was completely unaware as McCoy flew at him. At the very moment that he was finishing, "Do not budge!" McCoy hit him.

Peter's legs flew up into the air. His hands clutched at the sky as he lay prone three feet off the ground. Then gravity insisted upon its rights and Peter fell to the ground with a crash that knocked the wind out of him. Tristan gasped in surprise. Peter gasped for air. He and Peter stared at the fading wooly rump as McCoy streaked away. What Peter had taught, McCoy had wrought. And this was the only time I can recall when Peter ever budged. His steadfastness of spirit served him well where it mattered the most. No better champion than he when truth, justice and the American way were being threatened.

Solid as a Rock!

TRISTAN

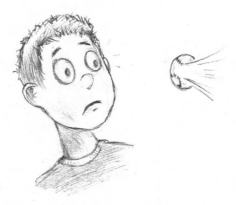

Tristan trailed Peter after three years. There probably wouldn't have been a three-year gap if there hadn't been a major advance in childbearing technology at the time. At least, that's what I thought in my young mind when Mom said she had had a "miscarriage." As in all technological leaps forward, there were mishaps, and two of our siblings never did arrive.

As Mom had said, "They missed the carriage."

But how can one blame those storks? For many centuries, they had been used to slipping their beaks through a baby blanket just under the knot and, with a good launch, getting right to the job and delivering the baby. Perhaps they would be a bit early if a great tailwind blew or a bit late if there was a strong headwind. But the baby was always signed, sealed, and delivered.

New means of transportation must have been developed and tried. And why not? Perhaps the efficiency experts decided to skip the blanket-carrying stage and slip the baby right into the carriage? I suppose it must have worked some of the time. To this day, I sometimes get a new- baby arrival card, and, sure enough, there's a stork carrying a baby carriage looped over its beak. Scant respect for tradition, it seems to me! Anyhow, two of our little family members missed a carriage, one between Leo and Marisa and one between Peter and Tristan. Twice the family planners must have tried one of those carriages and both times the siblings missed their ride. I'm not sure those planners have it right yet; the old blanket/stork method seemed to result in six, maybe, twelve good, safe deliveries—and that used to make for big, robust families. Now, families are lucky to get two or three children on the ground. Carriages must not be quite as dependable as Storks, my young mind figured. Some things just shouldn't be changed. But, just as new arrivals consoled Mom's heart after her first miscarriage, so did Tristan after her second.

Tristan was a little tyke. He sported the biggest brown eyes you ever saw, and he was so cute that past troubles had to be swept away to make room for new joy. On two occasions, those big eyes impressed themselves on to my memory.

Once, my grandparents on my father's side came

up from California to visit us. This was a very rare occasion and so very special. Grandpa was well into his sixties, a city dweller and a pharmacist by trade and we figured he wouldn't be able to play with us much on our country playground. But we had misjudged him badly. First, we showed off by doing chin-ups on the swing-set bar. He did five! We then went into the field, staked out a baseball diamond, and played a few innings. Grandpa could still hit and run. We were impressed—and Tristan got impressed in a way he will never forget.

Tristan was about six years old and was pitching. It was Grandpa's turn at bat. Tristan pitched and the ball made a beautiful arc as it sailed over home plate.

Grandpa swung hard and the bat swung true. It smacked that ball in a beeline for Tristan's left eye and caught him there before he even had time to react. It knocked him off his feet and he began to cry. He immediately grew a huge lump around his eye and it began to swell shut. We rushed him into the house to Mom where she put ice on it. Wow, did he end up with a shiner! It was as if his eye was a target and Grandpa shot straight.

Now, there are two ways that you can hit a target. Either the target is small and you're a really good shot; or the target is large and you're a lousy shot. In this case, I rather think that if Tristan didn't have such large eyes, Grandpa's shot would not have been so true.

The other way I remember those eyes was when they were the reason that the girl I had a crush on in eighth grade actually spoke to me. It happened like this. There was a rummage sale in the auditorium below the school where there were tables lined up in long lines loaded with all kinds of items. The tables ran parallel to each other with not much room between them, and I was working my way down one of these makeshift aisles with Tristan when I noticed Anne moving towards me in the same aisle! Could we and she meet? I began not to be to able concentrate on what I was looking at. My collar suddenly began to feel a bit too tight. Why the school principal decided to turn the thermostat up higher at this precise moment I have no idea. But it was decidedly getting much hotter. My breath began to labor torturously. She moved closer down the aisle until she was right there. Two or three feet from me at most!

In a portrait of a fish out of water and me, we would have looked just like twins. I gulped hard in an effort to say something nonchalant. But I only managed to wheeze out a pitiful "Hi!" I tried again to croak out something arresting to slow her progress, anything to keep her from slipping away. In a meeting that could have convinced her I was a bumbling idiot, Tristan saved the day. He was in first or second grade and was gazing up at Anne with those huge brown eyes. She looked down at him and then up to me and said "What beautiful big eyes!" I don't know what mine looked like peering from my beet red face, but I wagged my head up and down vehemently in total agreement. Tristan and his big brown eyes became a subject of common interest and we exchanged small pleasantries which I cannot recall. Everything just seemed to swim around in the confusion of my love-besotted mind. She left me in a euphoric state, and only a few more encounters with my love- never-to-be took place before we left each other for separate high schools. But Tristan's eyes turned what could have been an awkward encounter into a pleasant boyhood memory.

DAMIEN

Damien was delivered into the world the fourteenth child. I have been made to understand that the stork that had delivered us up to that time retired after that flight. His beak, back, and behind must have gone out of alignment. As big as Damien was, a carriage and ground delivery may have been more suited for his arrival. Given his size at delivery, I don't know how he fit between Tristan and Jessica, being just eleven months after Tristan and sixteen months before Jessica. It probably just got too cramped in there and he threw a fit and got his way with Mom. He was an expert at that and probably got a good young start at it. But it was not so easy with Dad.

"Damien is dying, Damien is dying!" Jeremy, Jake, and I screamed as we ran toward Dad. We had been playing cowboys and Indians up by the woods that afternoon. In the heat of the battle, one of us had noticed Damien rounding the corner of the house. He was reeling around like a drunken sailor and was as blue as Paul Bunyan's ox. Daddy, raking gravel on the driveway, paused long enough to look over at Damien to see what the matter was, and to our utter dismay, he went calmly back to raking. We were flabbergasted. As we pulled up by Dad, we were just a few steps from Damien, and sure enough, he was not going to last long. His eyes were clenched shut, his face was scrunched up—he seemed ready to burst.

Surely, we thought, choirs of angels will be coming to waft him away. He was teetering on the brink of collapse. Stunned, we stood there gaping. Where was Dad?! Man, if we were choking or in any other mortal danger, Dad would act so fast, either whipping us upside down, yanking us sideways, or otherwise upending us so that our heads would nearly fly off. Here, only seconds away from Damien's Armageddon, Daddy was serenely smoothing the driveway!

As we looked on in mounting panic and total dismay, Dad said calmly, "He'll be okay; he's just throwing a fit."

"But ... but ..." we spluttered as we caught our breath. "What's happening to him?"

"He's just holding his breath," Daddy explained.

"Sometimes a child can hold his breath until he passes out. He can turn mighty blue from lack of oxygen, but he can't hurt himself. He'll just start breathing again and be fine. He'll stop doing it if he doesn't get any attention for it; that's all he wants."

Well, Damien didn't pass out, and he stopped his fit when he found that all the attention he had garnered was dissipating. We watched a few more minutes as our blood pressures plunged back through the stratosphere and settled near sea level where they were supposed to be. Seeing that Damien was fine, we skipped back up to our battleground and commenced fighting. But I knew it had been a close one. *That* little brother was going to need some watching.

JESSICA

Jessica must have shut the door on her way out. There weren't any more children to follow. There was a span of twenty-two years between when Louisa was born and Jessica arrived. With so many storks coming in over the years, it's a wonder there weren't any mishaps besides the two who missed their carriages. All arrived in the best of health and vitality—and Jessica was no exception.

As Jessica soon found out, there were advantages to being the last to arrive. Whenever she got into trouble and was going to be reprimanded, by the time Dad got through all the names trying to remember which name lined up with Jessica, he was so exhausted that his consternation had dissipated and Jessica walked away none the worse for wear. Usually it would go like this:

Scene I: A very young Jessica puts a nail in the electrical outlet for the thirty-fourth time after having been told thirty-three times not to do it.

Scene II: Dad walks into the house to find Jessica putting said nail into the socket for the thirty-fourth time.

Scene III: Dad yells rapidly, trying to stop Jessica and shouts, "Loui— Elizabe—I mean Marisa! No, Rose!"

Scene IV: Mom runs into the room at Dad's first "Louisa," thinking he was calling her (I forgot to mention she's also named Louisa). She finds Dad spluttering out girls' names as fast as he can, losing his breath quickly. In desperation, he hurls out a "Cecilia!" hoping it will stick. With the last of his breath, and having now arrived at the baby's side to stop her, he says, "Jessica," more as a sigh of relief than a reprimand. He sweeps her up into his arms and collapses into a chair.

Ah, to be the baby of the family!

JEREMY'S TERRIBLE MEMORY

Jeremy's memory began to fade when I was six or seven. His memory loss became more apparent the older we got. The difference was subtle at first. At six, we remembered things pretty much alike; if I said I shot twenty enemy soldiers with my rubber bands and he said I shot twelve, why should I quibble? Our world was small then, and such little discrepancies were easily dismissed. Later, though, if I was to recount that I had shot the eye out of a vole that popped its head from its hole at fifteen feet away with my peashooter, but Jeremy maintained that my story was a little exaggerated, how could he be excused? How could he possibly, in the midst of dangling our trophy vole carcass in front of our sisters, stick to such a benign story as saying that we caught it by lifting up a board and snatching it from its home? Jeremy's awareness of the facts was clearly slipping. Now, some anomalies could probably be explained by the magnitude of the exploits themselves, as they were at times quite fantastic and dazzling, and Jeremy, when dazzled, could hardly be blamed for being discombobulated.

In spite of his memory lapses, Jeremy's companionship was my constant delight, and he figures prominently in my memories. The other fourteen siblings enter and exit the stage as they play their parts, but my recollections of them will be woven in here and there.

It would be immodest of me to attract too much attention to myself in relating our adventures together, but to make sure you also delight in them as much as I did, I will pop in when required. I will sometimes give Jeremy's recollection of these events in case he had something to add that I, in my modesty, forgot.

A fair warning as you follow these tales: there may be some small differences detected between my accounts of the events and Jeremy's. His accounts are a little fantastic and hardly believable when put up against the sober and measured telling of my stories. However, as I said before, his memory has beguiled him. I must stick to the facts, and so I will relate these events without exaggeration or embellishment, recounting them just as I saw them happen.

DAD, A CANOE, AND A BRIDGE

Eloika was a small lake located thirty miles north of our farm. It had the perfect ambiance for canoeing. Jeremy and I would slap the canoe onto the top of the car and jet up to the lake for a day of chasing turtles, catching fish (i.e., drowning worms), catching bull-frogs, or just enjoying the beauty.

Now, the most amazing thing about this lake was that there was absolutely no noise. The only way we could tell the difference between the regular frogs and the bullfrogs was by the size of their horns. I could hear fine when we left the house. And it was no problem hearing as we traveled up the driveway.

"Did we forget anything?" I would ask Jeremy.

"Naw."

"How about the worms?"

"Thought you had them."

"I put them on top of the car when you were tying on the canoe."

"Tying on the canoe?" Jeremy replied, eyes big with panic. "I thought you did it."

I hadn't tied it on. Jeremy always took care of that. I almost broke my neck as I twisted around to see if the canoe was lying on the driveway behind us.

"Just kidding—I tied it on," Jeremy laughed.

"Man, you about gave me a heart attack," I said as I swallowed hard to get my Adam's apple back down firmly in my throat. Color returned to my face as he stopped the car anyway. "What are you stopping for?"

"Guess those worms are still on the top of the car," he said, "unless they weren't holding on with both hands." I chuckled at the thought of worms desperately holding on to the rooftop with both their hands. How would they get their hands out of the tomato can to grip the roof, anyway?

We popped our heads over the car roof to see if the worms were still there. They were. Lucky them! No hands gripping the car. Their hands were still very much in the can. I was sure their hands were fully employed as they clutched their throats trying to stop their Adam's apples from shooting too far up their throats. It must have been frightening for a worm to contemplate being scattered across the interstate at sixty miles an hour. It's probably almost as frightening as the thought that a worm could contemplate at all.

We moved the worm can into the car and continued down the driveway. We talked until for some strange reason conversation became almost impossible. Jeremy would turn onto the interstate and begin to accelerate, slowly at first, and then faster. As we increased speed, there would be a low whistle, then a louder hum, and then an almost earsplitting whine. The whine would fade as we neared the lake and then would disappear altogether as we swung into the little gravel lot near the boat ramp. There, only blessed silence greeted us. People really meant it when they would say, "Let's go up to that beautiful lake; it's so quiet."

Thirty years later, Jeremy tried to confide the secret of the silence to me. As Jeremy and I started down that very same driveway with a different canoe but the same boat racks, he said, "Still haven't plugged the ends of those boat racks."

As we gained speed and as his voice got ever-dimmer, I thought I heard him say that the wind whistling in the ends of those hollow boat racks set up such an awful whine that he'd be almost stone-deaf by the time we reached the lake. For all those years, I thought we were in the presence of a natural wonder. But, no, the whistling in the hollow ends of the boat racks so deafened us that by the time we reached the lake our ears were completely numb. Stone-deaf!

Jeremy and I had taken this trip many times, and

this time we were taking our Dad. We weren't going to drown worms this time. We were going to try to navigate a canoe upstream against the strong current and had entreated Dad to lend us the use of his muscles with the off-chance that he might enjoy the outing.

As the snow melted upon the mountain tops and flowed its way down the mountainside, it formed a river which fed the lake on the north end. Jeremy and I would canoe up this little river as it meandered through slough and meadow. As the river got higher, it gave way to a swifter current and then to outright rapids. In the past, Jeremy and I had struggled as hard as we could to ply ourselves upstream to see how far we could get. Why? Because it was there, we had a canoe, and we were boys.

Paddling furiously, we would hit the rapids head-on. Jeremy would yell, "Watch that rock!"

Wait. Of the 1,142 rocks that Noah's flood had left strewn on this river bottom, exactly which one was I to watch? There was the one to the right that looked as if it had a nice left hook that could tear out that side of the boat. There was the one to the left that still seemed to be grinning from the last boat it had bested. Or, of course, there were the bluish-green ones that seemed to have been deposited everywhere for our viewing pleasure. From my perch at the front of the boat, I would elect to enjoy the scenery. But maybe because it was his boat, Jeremy never thought voting was appropriate, so he would invalidate my vote to enjoy the scenery, which would leave me flailing my paddle with increased effort to avoid the menacing rocks that continually sprang up in front of me. I was placed at the front of the canoe. Not only because of my ability to steer the canoe from there, but, more importantly, for safety purposes. In those days, our shirt buttons were made of steel. When my muscles bunched under my shirt in a Herculean effort to propel the boat forward, the buttons of my shirt would occasionally pop off at such velocity that they became dangerous projectiles. However, Jeremy said that I had to sit in the front because I was so skinny and I would often fall out of my shirt between the buttons and Dad and he would have to try to pull me out of the water—if they could distinguish me from the other twigs floating on the water.

What gave some help to our efforts was that at some points the water would become shallow enough that we could dig our paddles into the bottom of the river. This allowed us to propel ourselves forward and then to plant our paddles in the bottom to keep the river from forcing us back downstream. This was relatively simple in theory, but Jeremy could never seem to get it right. How else could I explain why every time I would put my paddle into the water we would go in the opposite direction to the one I intended?

At times we would get our little brothers to help us. But I soon discouraged this, as my story of Jeremy's ineptitude lost its effectiveness when the tale was retold by them. It seems that they thought I was a little remiss in my post in the front—and we couldn't have that kind of mutinous slander!

This time, though, we invited our Dad. Now, Dad

was one of those men who were as strong as an ox, and it was only rarely that he required my help for anything.

For example, Dad once built a farrowing shed for one of our sows. It was nice; it had four walls, a wooden floor, and was quite the maternity ward for a pig. Dad had to push this shed about forty yards up to where he wanted to place it. It was heavy; I was about six or seven and Dad had already begun to recognize my strength and how it might be best put to use. He placed me, my sister Cecilia (for decoration purposes only), Ivan, and the other three boys into the shed on the shiny wood floor. We all lined up along the front wall with our arms against the wall, ready to push. He told us, "When I say 'Push,' push as hard as you can on the wall." He then took Jeremy around to the back of the shed to help him push from there.

On the count of three, he said, "Push," and so we did. Cecilia, Ivan, I, and the rest of the gang pushed with all our might against the front wall from the inside, and Dad and Jeremy pushed with all their might from the outside. Sure enough, the shed began to move. As it gained momentum, Dad would remind us to push as hard as we could. We scrunched up our little faces in concentration and really laid into that wall. How I was able to sustain enough energy to push that shed those full forty yards, I don't know. Dad and Jeremy were sure breathing hard when we finished, but I didn't even break a sweat. It sure would have been nice if Jeremy had pushed from the inside with the rest of us kids where he could have done some good. Oh, well! Dad and I had pushed that shed and a handful of kids all the way up to the pasture, where it still sits to this day. I bet Dad was sure glad I was there to help.

He used this setup repeatedly when he needed my muscle. When the car would get stuck in the snow, he would put Mom behind the steering wheel of the car and me (along with the rest of the kids) lined up behind the front seat to push on the back of the seat to help get us out. Boy, did it help; Dad could push us out of most anything with help like that.

But back to the canoeing. I was in the front of the canoe, Dad was firmly ensconced in the middle, and Jeremy in the backseat.

The sensation of riding in the canoe in this way was remarkable. Jeremy and I would put our paddles in the water, and the canoe would move forward at a nice two-knots pace. But when Dad's paddle went in, we would be launched backward in our seats as the canoe streaked forward at forty knots. When Dad's paddle would come out, the canoe would immediately recede to three knots. Just as Jeremy and I would scramble back to our positions and attempt to paddle again, we would be launched once more from our seats, desperately trying to grasp any available handhold to avoid being thrown overboard. We would again claw back to our perches, only to be thrown off again. We lurched and faded, lurched and faded in this awkward fashion until we reached the mouth of the river.

We arrived at the rapids a little rattled but not too much the worse for wear, and we prepared our attack.

The idea was to keep the nose of the canoe going straight into the oncoming torrent; otherwise, if the boat would turn a bit sideways, the current would catch it and swing it around broadside and attempt to throw us over.

Having Dad in the canoe considerably changed the dynamic of our attack plan. When we were alone, Jeremy and I would wrestle our way up the rapids, and although we were seldom successful, we at least looked somewhat normal, with the canoe pointed to the front at least ten per cent of the time. Both our paddles would be in the water, waiting to seize the advantage when the water would be shallow enough to stick them in the riverbed. Between my prodigious effort and Jeremy's feeble one, our progress averaged out to a mediocre one.

Things worked a bit differently when Dad was with us. His paddle would hit the bottom, act like a fulcrum, and the whole canoe would rise out of the water in a beautiful arc, reach a zenith of the length of Dad's paddle, and descend with a splash down onto the water. What a spectacle: the canoe suspended in midair, high atop Dad's paddle, Jeremy's and my paddles pumping high above the water. The bullfrogs stopped in mid-croak to take in this startling scene. Eventually, the bullfrogs would give up any pretense of trying to get out a respectable croak and would be reduced to quivering masses of frog fat as they laughed themselves into convulsions and plopped off their lily pads.

This canoe-trip-cum-carnival-ride would have

continued indefinitely had Dad's paddle not decided it had endured enough abuse and broke in two. Jeremy's and my pride was partially restored when our paddles could once again reach the water.

With the combined effort of the three of us, we finally arrived at calmer water upstream. We navigated around some obstacles until we couldn't continue any further. We went for a walk farther up the creek and then returned to the boat for our ride back down with the current.

Now, one of the obstacles we had navigated around was a small wooden bridge that spanned the creek about two inches above the surface. Not two *feet* as Jeremy would later claim, but two *inches* at most. The exact height notwithstanding, we had to shoot back down the river under this bridge.

As we started downstream, my feet hung lazily over the side of the canoe, my toes dragging in the cool water. I hunched musingly in my seat, my paddle resting lightly on my knees as the afternoon sun lulled me into a half-sleep. We slipped smoothly down the river in this manner, soaking up nature's balm. My sixth sense, which was commandeered into duty because the other five had relinquished theirs, told me our speed was picking up a bit.

Sure enough, as I popped out of my gentle reveries and peered about, it was very evident that we were rapidly picking up speed. My mood changed from serenity to survival in an instant. We were gaining speed faster and faster as the current pushed us forward. Suddenly, the bridge appeared around a bend. We consulted whether we should jettison the boat and leap to the shore or try to go under the bridge by flattening ourselves as much as possible into the canoe.

We decided to stay with the ship. We didn't even have time to write letters back home. Two thoughts flew across my mind: (1) I was in the front and would have the most to lose if our judgment of getting under the bridge was faulty and (2) I could see the bridge flatten itself closer to the water as we made this insane attempt to shoot under it. When these two thoughts impressed themselves in my mind, I did the only natural, manly thing to do: I panicked.

My hat shot up as the hairs on my head stood straight and my eyes popped out from their sockets as they grew three times their natural size. Jeremy saw this look as I turned in terror and shouted, "We can't make it under!"

Seeing that my noggin was in mortal danger, Dad shouted back, "Get down, Nathaniel!" And, for once, obedience came naturally, and I flattened myself backwards into the bottom of the canoe. The bridge lowered itself even further trying to catch us.

We shot under the bridge at about 160, my nose leaving a grooved cut on its underbelly. You've never seen a bridge suck its belly up so fast in all your life. It just about broke its spine attempting to avoid my pointed nose. It now spans the river in a beautiful, high arc—a testament to the prowess of two boys, a Dad, and a canoe.

BIRDHOUSE WOES

Jake had a fervent wish to save Mom the trouble of chopping kindling. Utilizing his vast expertise on the home arrangements of the common bluebird, Jake would enthusiastically launch into the construction of a beautiful house for an expectant mother bird. Yes, it would always be an expectant mother. A mother expecting and expecting and expecting, but never getting. The reason for this discrepancy between expecting and getting was that Jake's eagerness to build for the bluebird kingdom was always equally balanced by his desire to provide our family with abundant kindling.

You see, we heated our sprawling farmhouse with a huge firewood furnace, consisting of a fifty-five gallon drum turned on its side and a conversion kit we purchased at the local hardware store. With the help of this kit, Dad turned a boring old steel drum into a fire-eating, and sometimes fire-breathing, heating machine. Obviously, a monster such as this required a lot of feeding. We spent many a fall day, and sometimes wintry ones, sawing firewood with a crosscut saw. After sawing, the wood would be hauled and stacked into piles of ample kindling.

The remarkable thing is that Jake was able to switch from his great concern for our feathered friends to a benevolent desire to provide the family with kindling in the blink of an eye. The concern was even more unusual as springtime brought forth the promise of warmth, not coldness. It also brought forth the bluebirds, who eagerly anticipated their springtime housing. Flying in, they would line up on their perches to watch as we plied our building trade. We built the birdhouses outside, either on the back porch or on the steps of the storage shed. This gave the bluebirds the choice between sitting on the branches of the silver maple or on the strings of the clothes-line to watch.

What, then, in the middle of springtime, would turn Jake's attention from building birdhouses to kindling? Oddly, it was usually just a little recalcitrant nail. Jake would be measuring, sawing, filing, and judiciously making sure every cut was just right. He would then squint down the length of every piece of wood to make sure it was plum.

Jake would then gather the proper nail into his hand, place it carefully between his thumb and forefinger, raise his hammer, and whack, the well-aimed blow would firmly implant his thumb into the wood. "Ahhh! Yiahhh!" With this gosh-awful sound, he would launch into the most fantastic of antics. Having thrown the hammer sixty feet across the yard and grabbing his mangled thumb, he would cut a fancy dance about the yard, all the while continuing to holler and yelp. After a few minutes of this, still sputtering some spells beneath his breath, he would search for his hammer.

As Jake parted the tall grass, Jeremy, barely able to control his laughter, would wink at me, saying that Jake was angry and was on the verge of saying things that might land him in the confessional. Nah, I knew better. I have it on good authority that Jake's antics were an ancient Indian dance, used especially in the construction trade. Jake had told me this in case I might express my fascination at his dancing and voluble vocabulary to Mom. His explanation seemed credible enough. I married an Indian gal since then, and she said her father was a mechanic and would indulge in similar dances at a moment's notice when his finger found its way into a piece of machinery.

Returning to Jake, after he found his hammer, he gingerly picked up the next nail with his now-modified thumb and forefinger. On the second attempt, eyeing the offending nail, he would take more careful aim. He would swing mightily, and the hammer would make a glancing blow, the nail bending defiantly. Intending to straighten the nail and pound it in at the same time, Jake would swing vigorously again. The nail, of course, would rebel and bend the other way. Jake, on the verge of another Indian dance, would swing even more robustly and miss the nail altogether.

This is when he would suddenly see the pressing need to abandon the expectant bluebirds and turn the wood into kindling. With repeated and ever-intensifying blows, he would reduce the partially assembled birdhouse into a pile of scattered kindling. Beautiful! Imagine him being able to transform his compassion for bluebirds into an endearing wish to provide kindling for Mom!

It never seemed to make much difference how far along Jake had proceeded in his construction of the birdhouse. I have seen him reduce a birdhouse to kindling before the wood even began to aspire to be a great house, and I have also seen him reduce a very fine example of a house to kindling even as the bluebird itself was picking out furniture and measuring for drapes.

On the other side, it became obvious to the bluebirds that if they hung their expectations on Jeremy instead of Jake, they could always rely on sturdy family homes built in a timely manner. I was a master builder, and Jeremy learned well under my tutelage. As long as he did exactly the opposite of what I did every step of the way, his houses turned out beautifully. Imitate me, and you had modern art—useless and ugly.

Jeremy fondly remembers the three of us building birdhouses together. Jeremy would try to mimic my carpentry skills as well as he could, with the aforementioned results, and Jake would reduce his to fine piles of kindling. Jeremy eventually caught on to building birdhouses that were the complete opposite of my example. His house is now laden with hundreds of birdhouses of varying shapes and sizes. Mine is also festooned with the birdhouses he built. Jake, I hear, is building a fine house for his wife. She has assured me she has no fear of being cold come winter. The house is still not quite complete, and the pile of kindling continues to grow.

Slingshot Rebellion

Pulling—that's what he was doing. There he was—the hunter drawing a bead on his prey. And what was this prey? A sassy mourning dove. Now, how can a bird with such a doleful name be sassy? Simple: put a ten-year old boy nearby with a slingshot pointed at it. That was all it needed to be justified to sound a cheerful note. Ten years old? Pluth! You could practically see the bird thrum its tongue, lift its wings, puff up its chest, and dare the boy to bean it. *That* boy was Leo.

Leo carefully aimed at this particularly cocky mourning dove. Now, this slingshot was not of the style that David used against Goliath. No, this one was of the forked-stick variety with two rubber straps. These finely-crafted slingshots were made of a very rare wood called fiberglass and were modified from the typical forked-branch model. It looked like a U with a handle hooked to the bottom. One held it in the left hand while pulling a suitable rock from one's pocket with the right. After placing a stone with his right hand into the pouch, a boy was all loaded up and ready to shoot.

The bands were surgical rubber tubes that were attached to the slingshot handle by being slipped over two metal studs protruding from the slingshot U. The tubes on my slingshot were about half an inch in diameter and required He-Man-like strength to pull. Jeremy's was about a quarter of that diameter. Leo's was somewhere in between, something more suitable for him to pull. I was able to launch a rock 270 yards or so at full draw. When Jeremy draws this statistic from his memory, he gets 27 or 28 feet, but it is so easy to drop a zero when dredging things up from the memory. Anyway, over time, the surgical tube on our slingshots would develop small stretch holes at the end of the studs. These would enlarge after great use and would snap under tension.

Leo had gone through all the necessary rituals to get off a particularly wicked shot.

As he eyed the dove with unwavering intensity, hoping to wilt the bird's courage, he groped around in his pants pocket until he found the perfect stone. After drawing it out of his pocket, he slowly turned it around in his fingers to position it in the slingshot pouch; it had to feel just so to make a good shot. Next, he slowly raised his slingshot to the perfect position. The insouciant bird was now fully framed by the slingshot. Leo instinctively sighted down the rubber tubes as he carefully drew back. With one last effort, he pulled back a little further, his tongue screwed into the side of his mouth with concentration, and whap! The slingshot rebelled. It let loose one of the torn rubber tubes from the handle and ferociously nailed Leo in the right eye "Yow!" he hollered as he commenced with a fantastic, spastic Indian dance of his own.

Indian dances were common in those days with us boys. Leo preferred to dance with his hands held firmly over his eyes, yelping and hollering all the while. During this dance, the bird laughed himself silly and flew wobbly on its way.

I, too, experienced a slingshot rebellion once. I was drawing a bead on a cougar right out past the spring-tooth harrow (a piece of farmer's equipment) in our field. I needed to pull my slingshot to the maximum, as a weak blow might make the cougar angry. Having the same revolutionary spirit that Leo and Jeremy's slingshot had, my slingshot let loose its fury and creamed my right eye. Not only did I see stars, I danced among them and saw all kinds of colorful galaxies in my paroxysms of pain.

Jeremy would say that I broke the handle of my slingshot by slamming it against the steel spring-tooth harrow in anger. But oh, no! My Indian dance required such fantastic antics that I accidentally struck the harrow. And Jeremy also claims that it wasn't a cougar I was shooting at, anyhow, but a house cat. Now, if his shrinking memory can turn a cougar into a housecat, what might he say about my alligator hunt? That I was catching four-inch blue-tailed lizards?

This is one story that, when retold by both myself and Jeremy, seems to coincide in most respects. There is a bit of slippage in Jeremy's memory, perhaps, but this adventure happened when our memories were better than those of our elders—and we were not yet deceived by people who claimed to stick closely to the facts. Certainly not when I could remember at five years old so clearly the way things really were.

INDIAN BONES

The elders in question were my two oldest sisters. Now, all of you know that older sisters lack the keen observation and acuity of senses that little boys have. They really were quite old at that time—sixteen or seventeen, at least—and at this age, older sisters seem to think that they know absolutely everything, when, in fact, little boys know that they know absolutely nothing.

All you have to do is ask older sisters a few simple questions: What's the difference between a frog and a toad? How short can you clip grasshopper's wings before it can't fly at all? Of course, these are simple questions to anybody but older sisters. It's different with older brothers. Everybody knows that older brothers know absolutely everything. They can tell you how Dan Frontier could subdue two Indians simultaneously while tied up and recovering from nineteen tomahawk wounds. They know that rivers are warmer the farther they are from the mountains because of the friction of the water on the rocks. See, they know these things. All you have to do is ask them.

When Leo and Andy, my two oldest brothers, were thirteen and fifteen, they discovered something extremely rare and were encouraged that Leo had read about exactly the same kind of thing in his cowboy books. This was the discovery of a pile of Indian bones right next to the woods behind our property.

In their excitement, Leo and Andy rushed to Jeremy and me to tell us of their discovery: "Jeremy, Nathaniel, Come quickly!"

"What? What?" we yelled as we jumped up from our toy trucks.

"We found a pile of Indian bones!"

We ran in eager anticipation to this amazing discovery as they waved us frantically towards them. They knew not to deceive us. We would have discovered subterfuge immediately if they had tried to pass these off as belonging to the Algonquin tribe, when everybody knows that Geronimo and his warriors were the only Indians who lived in the Pacific Northwest. But as they said by the sheer size of these bones that they must have belonged to a very tall and fierce Indian like Geronimo, we knew they were telling the truth.

I could positively tell that if the bones weren't Geronimo's, they were at least his brother-in-law's. How did I know this, you may ask? Easy: Indians sometimes wore their ribs on the outside of their clothes. And these bones were huge. They were so big that someone might think that they were deer or buffalo bones, but one could clearly see from the pictures in books that the Indians were really big and wore their ribs on the outside when they prepared to fight. These bones were just like those Indian bones, and, boy, were we excited. We oohed and ahhed and picked them up gingerly, with Leo and Andy pointing out the size and heroics of this particular Indian brave. As there were chips on the bones, Leo naturally said they were caused by cowboy bullets. Andy expounded by pointing out that six shots were obviously from Colt 45s and the other eight were from a .33 Winchester, probably John Wayne's.

Gosh, this Indian truly was a hero. We couldn't wait to spread the good news, so we ran excitedly to Louisa and Elizabeth. Now, I ask you, would you, when informed of this incredible and rare find, look at us with disgust and tell us to go play? That Leo and Andy were just kidding, and that the discovery was just an old pile of cow bones? Cow bones! Couldn't they see the bullet holes? Hadn't they seen Indian bones before? How, when you have the very evidence before you, could you presume they could be anything other than Indian bones? Had they not seen the pictures of Indians wearing their ribs on the outside? Did they really think that boys of Leo and Andy's experience, reading, and understanding could mistake cow bones for Indian bones?

After remonstrating with them for a few minutes and being convinced that they had no knowledge of important things, we took ourselves outside. Somehow Andy and Leo didn't come in to defend their find to the girls. Perhaps they were busy looking for a Viking ship in one of the ponds in the old mine.

THE GREAT CARP CAPER

One morning, Jeremy and I started out to subdue the great white carp. Captain Ahab going after Moby Dick had nothing on us. The waves were a good five feet high as we pushed against the west wind. I took the front of the canoe, as from there my shoulders could shelter Jeremy from the angry blast of wind. Water sprayed us with fury. We were scant, and we were scrawny, but we were determined as we clove our way through the waters.

We rode our narrow round-bottomed canoe much as a bronco rider rides a bronc. Jeremy flailed somewhat wildly at the surface of the water to push us along, as my blade bit deep into the river and thrust us manfully forward into the raging waters. Our destination lay at the other side of the lake. There, in the quiet water of the protected shore and small islands, lurked the carp.

We had armed ourselves with bow and arrow and were determined to bring some of the monsters home. I had a bow with a draw weight of about 130 pounds. I didn't have the exact specification, but I could tell it was around 130 because it was sort of hard for me to pull. Jeremy had set his bow gingerly in the bottom of the canoe so as not to break its fragile limbs. Although he said he had shot carp before, I much doubted it looking at his pathetic archer's tool. But if it was all he could muster, then who was I to discourage him?

What should have taken us four hours to get to the other side took only one, due to my brawn and some instruction to Jeremy on how to handle a canoe from the rear. Everyone knows that the control of the canoe is properly delegated to the man in front. I know this because Jeremy tried to tell me what to do from the rear, but it only resulted in erratic, zigzagging motions. So, after having traversed a somewhat zigzagged path across the lake, we arrived at calmer waters on the other side.

There we refined our strategy. The idea was to

glide very slowly and quietly among the lily pads and other surface flora of the river. The carp would feed on the decaying plant growth. Sometimes we could even hear the sucking sounds as the carp fed on them. At times we could see the scaly yellow back and dorsal fin of a carp exposed above the surface. These were choice shots, as one didn't need to shoot below the surface to nail one. Our arrows were attached to a string that unwound from a bow reel so that stuck fish couldn't swim away. Often we would be able to see the fish a few feet below the surface and a ways out. These shots required some real skill. Over time, we learned how much below the fish we had to shoot, because the refraction of the light from the water made the fish look closer to the surface than they were.

The waves were reduced to mere two-foot breakers when we arrived in the protected cove. Grizzly bear and other dispirited animals roamed the shoreline waiting for us to throw them a fish or, better yet, ourselves. Jeremy's faint heart did not allow us to get too near the shore, where the carp would feed up near the surface, so we stayed out in deeper waters.

The best way to get an angle on a fish was to have the archer (me) stand on the gunwale of the canoe in the front, and, as he sees a fish, he directs the paddler (Jeremy) in the back as to the speed and the direction he wants the boat to move. This could prove tricky at times, as Jeremy would usually be in the back of the canoe trying to extricate himself from a sandwiched position between the rear seat and the gunwale.

Anyway, as the boat rose and fell and bucked about,

I proceeded to arm myself with my bow and to climb onto the gunwale. A round-bottom canoe is not the most stable of ships, and, as it rolled and plunged, it was difficult to keep my knees from hitting my chin. Since I was so much better-muscled than Jeremy, even though he was my senior by one year, I put considerably more weight at the front of the boat. At this point, the bow was much lower in the water than the stern, and Jeremy looked a little ridiculous perched on his seat high above the water. His paddle would tap gently on the water as he attempted to reach the surface and directed the course of the canoe.

So, I found myself riding the gunwale; my hunting knife clenched in my jaws in case a great white carp tried to drag me into the deep and I had to dispatch him by hand. My eyes pierced the deep water, and we glided along the smooth—I mean the somewhat choppy—two-foot waves. Suddenly, off the port side, I spotted a carp. He was deep down, swimming along with a mean look in his eyes and fangs dragging from a curled lip. I whispered to Jeremy (so the fish wouldn't hear us, as fish can hear exceptionally well in the deep) to move the boat to the left. In characteristic hunting fashion, sensing the subtlety of the moment, Jeremy yelled, "What was that?!"

I had just released my hand from the knocked arrow and raised it to quell his outburst when he, thinking he now understood me, attempted to move the boat to the left, at which point we shot to the right. I was left with right arm raised, reaching for the sky and my right leg following suit. My left little toe was in a death grip on the left gunwale, and the bow was raised in a ridiculous display of homage to the sky.

Now, imagine what would have happened if I had lost control. As the boat rose on a huge wave, my left knee just grazing my chin, I deftly caught the strung arrow at the knock, drew back the full forty-two inch draw length of my 130 pound bow, and released the shaft at the fish. It was a little hard to piece together exactly what happened after that. What I saw headed for the fish was a sack full of lunch, a tackle box, three arrows, two pairs of pants, oars, and one of Jeremy's socks. In the violent lurch to starboard, the string on my professional reel, made from a genuine Heinz 57 tomato can, had fallen off in a heap on our pile of provisions, entwined itself in an impish way, and launched itself wholesale into the water. How it all squeezed through the hole I shot through the bottom of the boat, I can't say. Nevertheless, we managed to pull everything back up through the hole, although in a bit more imaginative way as they went in. After stuffing the hole with an old baloney sandwich scraped from the bottom of the canoe and holding it in place with duct tape, we continued to fish.

When I finally did get a fish, it wasn't that big of a deal. The wind had picked up a bit; the waves were now surging higher. Water sprayed in my face with biting fury. As I squinted into the spray and the setting sun, I spied a carp and he sighted me. As it feigned to the right, I adjusted my aim to head it off, and as it feigned to the left and lunged for the deep, I anticipated, drew back and shot under him. My arrow met him deep below the surface. Done quite easily—no need to adorn the tale.

Since Jeremy was my favorite companion, my affection for him could cause me to exaggerate when describing how he got his carp. After I had pulled out my ninety-pound carp into our nine-foot canoe, we switched ends. The water was a bit wild for Jeremy. Two-inch waves lapped plaintively on the side of the boat, and the gentle rocking was making me sleepy. Jeremy's knees knocked together as he clutched the bow tightly and peered fearfully over the gunwale, hoping not too big of a fish rose from the depths. Jeremy spied his trophy, drew back the full fifteen-inch draw of his twenty-five pound bow, creaking with strain, and let loose his toothpick—I mean arrow—at the fish. It struck home, and Jeremy pulled his trophy on board. I didn't have the heart to tell him that sunfish don't tend to grow over six inches. In the recounting the exploit, the fish would grow to a respectable two feet anyway, so why quibble?

Nighttime Milking

The job of milking the cows on our small farm fell to different children as our ages and circumstances changed. This responsibility eventually cascaded down to rest upon the shoulders of Jeremy and me, and so we found ourselves milkmaids in service of the family table.

At this point in time, we were milking two cows, both Guernseys. Pixie was the larger of the two and a little smarter than Pumpkin. They were owned respectively by Louisa and Elizabeth. We had hoped that they would follow their owners to their houses in the city, possibly as part of a dowry or something. To our surprise and consternation, these suggestions were summarily dismissed, and Jeremy and I were tied to these living milk bottles for the better part of three years.

As mentioned before, we had forty acres of land. The fifteen acres farthest from the house was divided off. This land was devoted to pasture and for raising grain crops. Our milking stanchion was a wooden platform with a system of wooden structures mounted on one end. When the cow put her head through the wooden structure to eat grain, they closed around her neck to secure it, lest she had any notion of escaping. On more than one occasion, when the latch failed to secure the cow, she would begin to back out of the stanchion while in the middle of being milked. This would provide the dog with much sport as we would try to milk the cow from an Indian-crouch position, shuffling along with a hop, lunging, grabbing the bucket, and generally losing all dignity in an attempt to keep the cow from stepping in the bucket.

A more romantic person might be envisioning a quiet, balmy, cool evening with birds chirping merrily, calves frolicking gaily in the pastures, Mom serenely hanging up the day's wash, and Jeremy and I tripping merrily along with our milk buckets to get to the placid, contented, and friendly family cow.

Oh, what could have been! In reality, we would

start out on our milking adventure about ten o'clock at night, having let it get pitch-dark outside and well past our bedtime. Mom would have told us approximately 296 times that it was time to go out and milk. We argued that the babies—at that time they were Tristan and Damien—were gaining too much weight and that a little less milk would be a good thing. Jeremy remembers our reasons being more that we wanted to continue playing with our toy soldiers, we were terrified of the dark, and we needed to go on teasing Rose. Well, we traipsed out the door one dark night to replay for the umpteenth time the following series of events.

The stanchion stood fifty yards or so from the house, or so it seemed during the daytime. During the pitch-dark night, that distance was much further—perhaps a quarter of a mile or so. We had our milk buckets ready to use as weapons in case any malcontent wildlife decided to test our courage. Why they thought they could intimidate us in the dead of night so armed, I don't know. We could clearly run faster, scream louder, and panic quicker than any courageous boy around, and that was before we were even warmed up. Once we fought off the clothesline and ended up running out into the dark and clobbering ourselves with the rake handle as it leapt up to whack us when we stood on its head, before we even arrived at the gate to the electric fence—or, rather, where we thought it could be found.

Now, how do you find the six-inch insulated handle of an electric fence in the middle of a dark night?

Easy! Eliminate all the other possibilities by putting out your hand and sweeping it back and forth while slowly moving forward until you either find it (this was the least likely and the least interesting), or grab the electric fence firmly and watch the sparks fly—or miss the fence entirely with your hands and run into it with the middle of your chest.

The last two options let you know that you hadn't found the handle, but they did not give you any particular clue as to where it actually was. You could tell how successful a milker was in discovering the handle by how well he glowed in the dark or how well his cap stayed down on his statically charged head. This time, Jeremy lit up to a brilliant white light as his metal milking pail pressed against the electric fence and I deftly caught the fence handle as he glowed. We quickly let ourselves through, as a boy only glows for so long.

You would think that the cows would be waiting patiently at the gate to be led into the stanchion because a nice couple scoops of grain waited for them to enjoy while being relieved of that day's work of changing pasture and water into milk. But, no, the cows were in the farthest corner of the fifteen acres—the farthest distance that they could be from the stanchion. They weren't standing there either. No, they would be sitting comfortably, chewing on their cud while Jeremy and I looked everywhere. We called out their names, not really hoping they would answer, but more to hear our own voices so we would not be overcome by fear.

We put our faces down near the ground, because you could sometimes discern a black mound rising from the ground. This would likely be a cow—but not necessarily. Sometimes it would be buffalo.

As we scoured the field for our bovine friends, we walked about fifty feet apart so we were more likely to bump into one of the cows. This usually resulted in some very interesting antics. Imagine me calling out with the strong and commanding voice of an eleven year old and Jeremy piping out in a squeaking and wavering voice, trying to lure a reluctant cow to give up her location, when a startled buffalo leaps up and thunders away with half the herd following. Usually this would require a fast retreat, as any respectable panic would demand, but this never happened for us. A panicked retreat requires a beating heart, a healthy flow of oxygen through the lungs, and extremely fast churning legs. But how can any of this happen when your heart is stuck in your throat and the sudden fearful gasp won't allow you to exhale? You just stand there frozen in fright. This inability to move is handy, though, because later when the story is retold, you can honestly say you stood your ground in an out-of-control buffalo herd in the middle of the night.

Well, despite threats of buffalo stampedes, we continued our fearful search for the cows. What was completely unfair during our expedition were the birds that conspired with the obstinate cows. We were moving cautiously along when suddenly a bird burst up from the ground and scared the living bejeebers out of us. I tried to follow Jeremy as well as I could as we tore across the field in terror. It's difficult to follow someone when you're in front of them, but I did my darndest. Jeremy claims I was leading because I was more scared than he was, but I was only being the brave one as I blazed a trail for him.

Unfortunately, we had to return to our search after we determined that a small feathered friend had caused our involuntary foot race. We laughed and assured ourselves that we weren't even scared and knew all along that it was just a bird. This helped us to buck up our nerves, and we set to our task again.

As we neared the edge of the far end of the pasture, we began to anticipate running into the barbed wire fence that enclosed that field. Trying to disentangle our clothes from the barbs in the dark usually resulted in the wire losing the battle, but it would leave enough scars to show that it had put up a good fight. The cows would usually recline as near as they could to this faithful ally.

When we finally did capture the cows, they refused to let us put their halters on. It was bad enough that we had to do everything by feel. The cows swung their heads from side to side, up and down, and anything else to evade the halter. Did you know that all cows have different names than the ones the owner originally gives them? Louisa and Elizabeth had named our cows Pixie and Pumpkin, but we were more apt to call them by their proper names: Stupid Cow, Idiot, Stop It Now, Knock It Off, and so on.

When we did finally secure the halters, we still had to get the cows to stand up. We pulled as hard as we could. Exerting the full power of my ninety-pound frame on the rope, I could coax Pumpkin to extend her neck in mild discomfort. But the cow remained fixed to *terra firma*. She would not budge.

Then came the begging and the pleading, and the bribing and bullying. Lastly came the reminder that hamburger was the food of choice for a large family. Suddenly, the cows were overcome by empathy. They practically exuded compassion for the plight of small children. They leapt up eagerly from their lethargic position, Pumpkin standing on both of my feet in her exuberance to get going, as she practically ran for the house. Jeremy had equal luck with Pixie. The toes on both of his feet were suitably mangled, and his cow started out at a great clip for the stanchion.

Cows can see reasonably well in the dark and can maneuver around the various pitfalls that waited to trip an unwary traveler. That left Jeremy and me hanging on for dear life as the cows ran pell-mell across the pasture. We had to do the best that we could, slipping and sliding on fresh cow pies, breaking our legs in gopher holes, and involuntarily playing crack-the-whip as the cows rounded the corners. Finally, we were jerked to an abrupt halt as the cows planted themselves in front of the electric gate, waiting to be let through to their supper of grain.

The search for the handle of the electric fence, if unsuccessful, was downright dangerous. And we misfired. Two cows, two boys, two lead ropes—all were electrified. Bedlam broke loose. Cows bellowing and bucking, boys banged around, trampled and squashed between two angry bovines. We finally found ourselves standing with Jeremy holding my cow, me holding his, me wearing one of his socks, he wearing one of my shoes, and me with my head out my sweatshirt sleeve and an arm out the neck hole.

After sorting out this mess, we once again attempted our exit. Of course, when we did undo the gate, the cows did not believe that the gate was not there after their prior misplaced trust in us. It took another whisper of McDonald's to persuade the cows to comply. At this, they shot through the gate and onto the stanchion floor and thrust their heads through the holding hole. Of course, we would always shut this ... except for when we wouldn't.

Sometimes we started milk fights in the dark, but since these usually left both of us a sticky mess without either of us being able to get an advantage, we saved those battles for the days when we began milking before dark. The cows would be standing parallel to each other, and we would shoot streams of milk at each other from our squirt guns but having the advantage of a whole cow to hide behind and a four-barrel weapon to fire.

Now, the cows did not always share our enthusiasm for this warfare and felt it was their duty to remind us that they were not to be abused by promptly kicking us in the shins. We would return to our milking after this gentle reminder with some equally gracious remarks on the cows' intelligence, finally having some milk to show for all our efforts.

ROOSTER

When I was about five years old, we owned a large white rooster that was the terror of our farm. This leghorn was born mean. Good breeding certainly hadn't provided him with a good disposition. Education, finishing school, gourmet food, and all the other amenities that we provided our entire barnyard menagerie only seemed to feed his distemper rather than soften him into a respectable member of the family. The egg he emerged from had either cracked prematurely or had gone rotten. Either way, it gave him a character that lacked any of the finer inclinations that might have led him to a life of virtue and profit.

This ornery old rooster stalked our farm with a haughty air and dared anyone to challenge his mastery over the farm. We kids had to draw up battle plans to evade his notice whenever we ventured outside the house. First was the furtive glance from behind the screen door as we slowly opened it to see if the rooster was in sight. Then came the slow, quiet sneak across the yard to get to the rabbit pens. Then we very carefully lifted the lid to the rabbit food, not making the slightest hint of a noise that might reveal our position. There was the gentlest shake of the food scoops as we filled each of the rabbit cages with food. The thought raced through our minds that if we could just make it through our chores without detection, we might live at least to the ripe old age of seven or eight.

Next came the hasty retreat back to the house. But there were at least thirty-one ways that our perfect plan might be foiled and land us in a fight for our lives. One, of course, was the big sisters. They would yell from the door, "Nathaniel! Mom said you have to come in right now to pick your army men up off the floor."

Now, it wasn't the army men part that upset me—they were right on the mark there. And I would need a whole regiment of army men as reinforcements if I were to survive the trip back to the house if that rooster spotted me. No, it was the timing of the reminder that doomed me. Leave it to an older sister not to recognize the mortal danger she was exposing her sibling to. Did she really expect me to yell out and give my location up after I had worked so hard to remain undiscovered? I figured it was best to try to get my sisters' attention by waving wildly. They didn't see. I tried doing a dance of wild contortions, pulling faces, and generally looking like a turkey in a conniption fit. None of this worked, though, because my sisters were hiding behind the screen door in fear of the rooster, too. There was only one thing to do: a quick vector and speed calculation to ascertain my chances of making a successful dash to the house. There were a number of things to consider: the distance to the house; my running speed; the rooster's attack speed; and last, but certainly not least, Dad's rescue speed.

I let my five-year-old mind process this data. Our farm was about forty acres, with our house situated in the northwest portion. Now, Dad could be working on any of the 250 million square inches of the land, and to determine which square inch he was on at any given moment was impossible to do. This was important—because our last line of defense was always Dad. If Dad could get to us before the rooster, we could get away ruffled, but alive. If not, the rooster got us, and we were beaten and sparred to within an inch of our lives. Now, when you're only five, there aren't many inches to your life, so they dwindled pretty quickly. How Dad always seemed to arrive so quickly still amazes us to this day.

But back to the story. On this occasion, I shot from

the starting block in perfect form, my eyes affixed to the back door, my little legs churning furiously, and my arms pumping madly as I raced for the door. The rooster spotted me as I poured on the coal; but I was a speed demon. The evil leghorn checked its compass, adjusted its angle, and commenced in hot pursuit. I began to scream loudly; my screams rose in pitch in direct proportion to the rooster's distance from me. His two large drumsticks pressed to full advantage as he came at me like a white locomotive. I tried felling him with a withering look as I caught his beady red eye in my sight, but this only fed his fury as he hurled himself recklessly at me. When I realized that I was not going to make it to the porch, I quickly turned to meet him face to face.

There were only two possible outcomes of this contest: I win or the rooster wins. My only hope was that Dad would get there in time. The rooster's only hope was that Dad wouldn't get there on time. I knew that if I could hold him off for just a few seconds, Dad would arrive, both barrels blazing. So I set to the task with gusto—the rooster with its nine-inch spurs and sharpened beak, and me with a size four shoe and a withering scream. There I was, both hands punching with all my might, my left foot planted firmly on the ground, and my right foot kicking at ninety strokes per minute. All I could see was a flurry of white feathers as he tried to peck with his beak, beat me with his wings, and slice me with his spurs. I fought with fury and shrieked with a will, and I had that rooster a bit flummoxed. It was only for a moment, though, as I only seemed to intensify his bloodthirsty intentions.

Jeremy said that this loud commotion lasted only a few seconds, but I knew that rooster and I were at it long enough to size each other up and come to an understanding: he betting Dad wouldn't make it and I trusting in the paternal instinct to protect the brood—even if it was a scrawny one like me, not worth much at auction, even soaking wet. Well, Dad did make it, and when he did, oh my! Dad came in low to the ground at about ninety miles an hour, intent on doing harm.

When the rooster saw him, it lost two of its own lives and three borrowed from the cat. It didn't have time to make its apologies or its will. Dad's size-twelve caught it in the chest and sent it into the next kingdom. The rooster saw its judgment flash before its eyes. How it returned to this world with all of its wits after that reckoning, it is not for us to know. Unfortunately, it never got religion, and it would be out stalking another one of us in short order.

Now, I'm sure you're thinking that this was my only encounter with the rooster. But, no. You see, we had a long and storied history.

About a day or two after this last encounter, Dad did the most unthinkable thing imaginable: he asked me to roust the hens out of the chicken coop. It was evening, just when the hens had settled on their roosts to gossip about the scandals of the day and cluck about how bad things were getting over there in the next barnyard, what with dogs and cats living in the same house and all. Now *I* was to enter this quiet, domestic scene and shoo them out! It wasn't so much that this rooster had a keen eye—all roosters do. No, this one could see around corners and hear things before they even made a noise, and to top it off, it could see from the back of his head. Some of you may have had teachers who had these preternatural powers and know what I mean.

To add to the challenge, this chicken coop was raised about three feet off the ground, and the chickens accessed it by walking up a ramp. The coop had a number of roosts in it. They started from high up in the back and descended down to the front of the coop. This left about two feet of space between the bottom roost and the front of the coop in which one could barely find room to stand. I had to climb up into this semi-dark cavern and try to gently coax about eleven hens to give up their comfortable sleeping quarters.

I tried to convince the old biddies that it was to their (and my) advantage that we do it in the greatest secrecy, and in perfect silence. A few muffled clucks and some light murmuring indicated to me that they were of the same mind, and so I gathered my courage and began to shoo them from the coop. What a mistake! First, I shouldn't have just screwed up my courage—I should have cemented it to me—because when those hens let loose their shrieks, courage slipped right out of the hole in the bottom of my pocket, rolled down my leg, and ran for dear life.

Having lost my courage, what was a coward to

do? I tumbled out of the coop and scrambled to my feet in anticipation of running. But no such luck! I was caught as naked as a jaybird in a jenny house. The rooster was already rushing over to see who had had the gall to mess with his hens. Fortunately for me, Dad also knew that the rooster would be mighty interested in finding out what was happening in the hen-house, and he came running, too. He met the rooster milliseconds before he was to give me a most thorough drubbing. When the rooster saw Dad and his size-twelve boots, his coxcomb sprang straight up, his eyes about popped from their sockets, and he turned around so fast that he left half of his feathers twirling in a whirlwind as he hightailed it to safety behind the pump shed. He never learned. We kids ran many a race with that rooster. We lost some and won some, and more often than not, Dad's size- twelve was our deliverance.

Four Below Zero

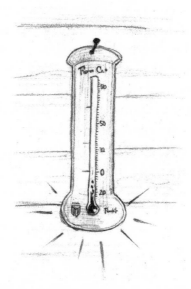

We grew up with an implicit trust in our elders and those in positions of authority, as any well-adjusted youngsters should. At times, however, this could cause us to be deceived by those who abused that trust.

We kids were avid outdoor sleepers and were often subjected to the vagaries of the weather. Most of our armament against this fickle power consisted of old blankets to wrap up in and old tablecloths to use as ground tarps. If these comforts were only enjoyed by us, we would have done well, especially if the temperature stayed between sixty and seventy with no wind or rain. The only problem, though, was that these old trappings were not our only company. The old tablecloths amplified every movement of ants as they made their nightly excursions to visit friends and stay up all night partying, ants being a sociable species.

Many nights were interrupted by me flying out of bed and snatching up my ground cover to catch the critter that was scratching at the underside of my makeshift bed. I came up empty every time, and it wasn't until early one morning when the new sun had just risen that I discovered these little hotshots were the ones responsible for my nightly scrambles from under the covers.

The old blankets also attracted a most unsavory bunch of hangers-on, rustled out of every weed patch within eighty-two miles. With burrs of every description coming in droves to take up abode in our threadbare covers, along with grass that had been rejected by more respectable blankets and, in general, any citizen of the plant family firmly attached to our covers, we could never enter the house without bringing a whole neighborhood of homeless weeds. Now Mom was a compassionate lady, but with fifteen of her own children, she frowned on us bringing a bunch of plant life for adoption.

Needless to say, this combination of weather and bad company made us determine that it was time to shake the old ways and enter the modern world of outdoor sleeping with an invention called a sleeping bag.

This would logically solve all the aforesaid problems. The sleeping bag weighed only seventeen ounces. It was six-inches thick all the way around, toasty warm, shaped like a mummy's wrappings, had outer shells made of all-natural man-made materials that shed all water, fended off any angry wind, and was like sleeping on a thick, warm cotton mattress. This was all accomplished by a magical space-age material called Dacron 88.

Jeremy and I were determined to acquire two of these incredible bags and took ourselves, with a little help from Mom, to the big sporting goods store called Yellow Front. Not only was the store *called* Yellow Front; the whole screaming front of the store was actually bright yellow. This might have been a marketing ploy, because every shopper was struck half-blind and the merchandise made to look wholesome by the bright yellow assault on our eyes when we entered the store.

Anyway, to make a short story long, we proceeded to the section that had oodles of these modern marvels, and we began our search for the perfect bag. They were hung from large hangers, and we plied through them methodically. But then it happened: the salesman appeared. At that time, we took salesmen at face value—say, four dollars and ninety-five cents. I don't know if their worth has gone up since then, what with inflation and all.

Jeremy had picked out a bag that suited his fancy. It was a green mummy bag made of some fiber whose name I don't even remember, but it was supposed to perform even better than Dacron 88, the material the bag I had chosen was made of.

We thought we had both made good choices and we must have, because it was a marvel to hear the salesman relate so many details of the products we had chosen and describe why our choices were perfect. Imagine, out of the other hundred or so sleeping bags in the store, we had chosen the best, and, to top it all off, they were on sale!

We weren't so surprised, though; after all, we were experienced outdoor sleepers and good judges in these matters. (Just how good will soon be discovered.)

For each of our bags, there was one key selling point. For Jeremy's, it was the incredible claim that the sleeping bag was rated toasty-warm down to four degrees below zero. Now, how in the name of Jim Bridger could the manufacturer claim this with such precision? Why not say down to say "two below" or "five below"? Did this rating mean that at three below one would be the picture of comfort, and at five below an icicle? We concluded that if science could make these precise distinctions, we were in for some very serious outdoor sleeping.

The selling point for mine was that it was not a mummy bag. My bag was the traditional oblong-shape. I opted for this because I preferred to sleep in the fetal position. You had to consider the advantages of this when you had to make quick getaways from the frightening noises of the night. You see, in the traditional oblong-shaped bag, when you lay in the fetal position, you could pull your knees up to your chin without disturbing the surface of the bag. This allowed you to get up to a sixty or seventy miles-an-hour running start without even leaving the bag. And when you did shoot out of the bag, your legs were already going at the desired speed. In a mummy bag, on the other hand, the bag hugged you from top to stern, and if you brought your knees up, the whole bag came with you. Now, this didn't leave you with any way of getting properly warmed up for your getaways because both legs had to work in tandem, much like in a gunnysack race. This mode of hopping might have the advantage of making a cougar laugh so hard it couldn't stand up, but it also had the distinct disadvantage of landing you on your nose at the most inconvenient times.

A few days after making our purchases and having convinced Mom that we certainly weren't afraid of sleeping out—as we were quite a bit older then, it being at least a whole week prior since we had burst into the house the last time we slept out—we took our bags to the backyard. No old tablecloths, no blankets, no pillows, and no sense—I mean, no cents.

SLEEPING OUTSIDE

Now put these four words together; *sleep, outside, eleven,* and *nighttime.* This does not equal "sleeping outside." This really should read, "Eleven-year-old boys shiver uncontrollably in fear until dawn."

Many would argue that sunlight is necessary for growth. Au contraire! How can a mouse be about three inches long during the day and grow into a large bear at night? Ask any eleven-year-old boy how many times he has witnessed this when trying to sleep outside at night. You will find very few dissenting opinions, and

I suspect that those opinions you heard were from less experienced outdoor sleepers, like ten-year-olds. They most likely would claim the mouse had grown into a cougar. Such mistakes can be excused in younger minds, but those of older vintage and greater experience knew that mice grow into bears at night.

How did I know this? Cougars and bears have distinct ways of sneaking up on unsuspecting eleven-year-olds. Bears tend to rustle as they sneak up on you, whereas cougars are inclined to crunch as they approach. To discern this required the utmost powers of concentration. Nerves stretched taut by the anticipation of inevitable attack, eyes bulging from their sockets, white-knuckled hands gripping the blankets firmly over the head, and ears at fevered attention provided this concentration.

Our jaws would be clenched tightly shut so that the rattling of our teeth would not give away our exact location. In a barely audible but obviously quaking voice, I would force out the words, "What was that?" The conversation would continue as follows:

"What was *what*?"

"*That.*"

"That *what*?"

"That *noise.*"

"*What* noise?"

"*That* noise!"

"I didn't hear any noise."

"Well open your ears!"

"They are."

"Do you hear it now?"

"No."

"Now?"

"No. It was probably just a mouse. Go to sleep."

"Go to sleep?" I would exclaim in horror. "I'm sure it was a rustle " (Now I would be certain it was a bear sound.) "Do you hear it now?

"No. Where?"

"Over *there*."

"Over *where*?" Jeremy would ask in a slightly more excited voice.

"Over *there*!"

But how was one to distinguish one direction from another when someone is insisting "over there" and both of our heads are buried under six feet of covers?

Any direction could have been "over there." For one to repeat the question "over where?" and the other to answer "over there" with an ever-increasing dread in their voices only increased the poignancy of the situation.

Who was going to be fool enough to poke his head out of his covers to ascertain just where the noise was coming from?

So the conversation continued in this most idiotic fashion:

"Did you say it was a rustle?"

"Yes."

"Are you sure?"

"Yeah."

"Didn't sound like it to me."

"Shhh! I heard it again."

"It's probably just Leo or Andy trying to scare us."

"No, they're gone."

"Oh, Yeah."

"All right, then. Go to sleep."

There it was again. "Sleep." Have you ever tried to sleep when it's pitch-dark outside and noises, clearly made by ferocious beasts, sound all around you? A person could wake up dead, and then where would he be? The shock of it could scare you to death. Imagine the headline: "Two Small Boys Wake Up Dead, Almost Die Of Fright!"

Well, sleep wasn't coming. It was probably too scared to get close to us. In any case, it was avoiding me. An older sister once made a suggestion to help with my outdoor insomnia. She suggested making the ground softer by carrying out more blankets or pads. How silly of her! To my knowledge, I never touched the ground the whole time it was dark outside. In my paroxysms of fear, I would pull one end of the covers so hard over my head, with the other end tucked securely around my feet, that I would pull myself up off the ground and remain suspended about three feet in the air. There I would be, quivering and suspended in the air, the blankets stretched to their breaking point. Because I still had not determined the source of the noise, I figured that I only had to hold this position for six more hours until daybreak.

With my nerves drawn as tight as a fiddle string— and thinking things could not possibly become more desperate—a malicious coyote would unleash its unworldly howl and set my heart on a pace that had to be measured in beats per millisecond. These howls consisted of the most gosh-awful sounds that a fevered imagination could conjure up.

They would start with an innocent yelp, morph into a high-pitched scream that sounded like two screeching banshees, build to a long pitiful yowl that seemed to reach back into mournful eons of loss and betrayal, and then end in a yapping, laughing cacophony. And this was just one coyote. When a whole pack of them started, they would raise such a din that all the dogs in the far reaches of the other farms would raise their voices in protest or sympathy.

Sleep was banished forever from the land, and an eleven-year-old boy would be seen streaking toward the house in terror. Yes, *streaking*. I would be lucky if I still had my Skivvies on after I shot out of my blankets. My pajamas usually trailed a few yards behind, as they didn't stand a chance of keeping up in my mad race to the door. This made it rather difficult to saunter in to your bed nonchalantly as all your sisters looked on, what with me naked as jaybird and my pajamas banging on the door to be let in.

"What did you come in for? You scared?" they would ask.

What a question! Just because my curly hair stood straight up, I was only in my Skivvies, and I was shaking from prow to stern, white as a sheet, why would they figure that an Indian brave by day would become a shaking, scared little boy at night? How ridiculous!

No, I would declare myself an official weather

prognosticator on the spot and announce the possibility of rain.

And who wants to sleep in the rain?

MY LEGS HURT

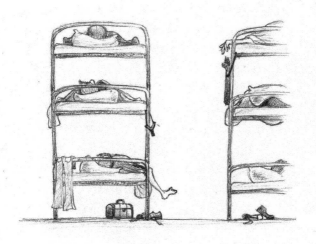

"My legs hurt": How many times did Mom and Dad hear those words cried out in the middle of the night? Oh, I'd say about 4,680. Fifteen kids have 30 legs split evenly among them. Leg aches begin at, say, a year and a half and can persist until the age of seven or so. Average one leg ache a week, and that's 52 per child for approximately 6 years. And 6 times 52 equals 312 in pre-self-esteem math and anywhere from 1,200–1,500 in post-self-esteem math. For the sake of tradition, let's follow pre. (Really, you *have* to follow pre because if you went before pre, you would be "pre-pre," and then where would you be? Wouldn't that make pre "post"? But that's preposterous!)

Well, 312 multiplied by 15 tykes is, as I was saying, 4,680. That's a lot of crying out. Mom and Dad were real troopers, though, and always answered our distress calls. They would drag themselves from bed and make a hasty calculation as to just how awake the response to this particular call would require them to be. If it was just a light whimper and a pitiful "mmyy lleegg hhuurrttss," then they could slightly open the door leading from the dream world to the real world. In this half-sleep, they would maneuver the maze of cribs and bunk beds until they found the offending limb. If the angels trod softly that night, they could administer relief and return to bed without losing too much precious sleep. Of course, if the call for assistance was a commanding "my legs hurt," then full engagement in the real world was required and sleep was swept away, hopefully to be found again before daybreak.

What made our leg-aching nights so memorable was the way that Dad and Mom approached these tasks of relief. Our little ears could always discern which of the two had been sent to answer the distress call. If it was Dad, there would be a whoosh as his bedcovers were thrown back, followed by the sound of a half-asleep man trying to navigate past all the crib legs that lay in wait to grab his little toe and give it a good stub. A muffled "Ah!" would mean that he had been bested. Mom would ask if he was all right. Silence meant he was fine but not happy.

If Mom answered the call, there would be a slight rustle and stirring as she quietly disengaged herself from the bedcovers. Next, there would be the sound of her hand patting the floor as she leaned over the side of the bed trying to find her slippers. The only problem was that more than likely her slippers would have been kicked under the bed by one of us as we passed by in the dark, and she would have to get down on her knees and fish around for them among the monsters under the bed.

A gentle sigh would indicate that she had gotten herself together. We would hear the light shuffling of her feet as she found her way to the sufferer's bed. Draping herself over the railing of the crib, she would ask us which of our legs hurt. We would tell her, and she would begin to rub our leg gently, back and forth, back and forth, back and forth, all the while struggling to stay awake as she drooped over the railing. Sometimes she would administer an aspirin with her soft mothering to ease our woes. Soon, these maternal ministrations would soothe us back to the land of chocolate and fairies. You might call hers the holistic approach: the combination of medicine, love, time, and attention. Who could argue with it? It certainly worked, and it was the approach most preferred by us patients.

Dad's was a decidedly different approach. It was certainly done for the same reasons—love, the alleviation of pain, and the desire to go back to sleep. But he had a much more scientific understanding of what caused a leg ache and attended to his task accordingly. He would wrap his huge hands around the calf of our leg and squeeze and release, and then he would move a little higher up, squeeze and release again, and thus, by repeating this sequence a few times, he would force blood up the leg. It really worked, too. As Dad squeezed, our head would swell with the rush of blood, much like the skin of a sausage being stuffed. Our head would then deflate to normal size, and Dad would repeat the process. We quickly learned to close our eyes tightly to keep our eyes from popping out of their sockets.

To this day, I don't know if it was the over-saturation of the brain that gave us a feeling of euphoria or if it was the relieving of the leg ache, but we sure did sleep well afterwards. Like I said, we preferred Mom's approach because with Dad's there was a certain amount of pain involved. We never knew when Mom left to return to bed, as we would be fast asleep by then. But after Dad's leg massages, he would ask if it hurt anymore. We would immediately say no, but would have to get back to him at a later date after the blood had redistributed itself in a more balanced manner. His whole administration of charity would be over in a matter of minutes, whereas Mom's could take a lot longer. Both were acceptable, but we preferred Mom's holistic approach to Dad's scientific and efficient method.

ELECTRIC FENCES AND ME

One summer, I got to raise a low-down, deceptive, skinny, mangy, conniving, and just plain worthless heifer as my calf. Now, how this bag of bones could have been the child of Millie, I can't imagine. I had raised Millie from a calf, and she had turned out to be a large, well-proportioned Angus cow that could hold her own in any bovine beauty pageant. She had thrown a beautiful bull calf the year before, and I waited with eager anticipation for her baby the next year. Well, the little heifer came out all right and looked to be getting a good start on the farm. But then something got into her that interfered with all things bright and beautiful and sent her down the path of all things dim and ugly. Yes, I know that sounds a little harsh, but even her momma stopped taking her to the herd revues because all the other matronly cows shook their heads in derision. So that is how I came to be the master of the little one. I named her Polly. The name, of course, conjured up a picture of a pretty southern belle, but all I got was a northern ding-dong.

That summer, we had a set of pens of various sizes about sixty yards from the house to the northeast. It was here that many of our pigs were housed and, at times, our cows as well. One of the sections of fence that Dad had built needed to be repositioned to accommodate our growing collection of beasts. This particular section was built with rails of one-by-fours and was about ten feet long and four feet tall—which made it about six inches taller than I was and a good deal heavier. Of course, at the advanced age of ten, I could wrangle cows with the best of the cowboys, but I had not yet learned all the tricks that a section of fence could devise. This one conspired with an electric fence that ran parallel to it about two feet away.

I walked up to the arrangement to see how I might devise a way to wrangle the fence off its feet, jog it out about a foot from its present position, move it forward a few feet, and secure it in its new position.

This was not too complicated when looked at from an armchair. But I wasn't in an armchair. I was at a distinct disadvantage.

As I eyed the wooden fence to see how I might move in quickly, grasp the bottom of the fence with my left hand, kneel on one knee, grab the top of the fence with my right, wrench it up with the element of surprise, and move it as described above, I could see the fence with equal cleverness saying to itself, "Now, if I can just get him to come in fast, drop to one knee, grasp me low with the left hand and high with right hand, I bet I could throw him."

You see, this fence had its foot planted firmly in the tall grass, something that I had failed to notice. I went in for the move. I dropped to one knee, grasped the bottom rail with my left hand, grabbed the top rail with my right hand, and lifted as hard as I could. Meanwhile, with a quizzical look on her face, Polly seemed to say, "This ought to be fun. This scrawny kid is going to move that fence?"

Well, I *did* move the fence. Right over on top of me! With its hind foot firmly planted on the ground, the fence lunged upward into the air and jumped on top of me. I was borne down to the ground and engulfed in its embrace. I was fairly certain that the fence had intended to pin me against the electric fence, but it was foiled by its own zeal. In its enthusiasm to get the better of me, it got itself slightly off-parallel, and when I fell over with it on top, the front of it caught the electric fence and brought that down, too.

Polly was simply tied in knots with delight when

she saw me upended and helpless. I did not share in her merriment. Quite the contrary, I was hollering at the top of my lungs for help. I was in the most precarious of positions, as the downed electric fence was just inches from my left ear. It was only with great effort that I was able to hold my head up to keep my ear from touching the electric fence. With the full weight of the wooden fence pushing the air out of me, hollering and straining to keep my ear from contact, I knew that time was short before my goose was cooked. The thought of a fried noggin was enough incentive for me to put out a dramatic distress signal.

One of the many advantages of growing up with a whole gaggle of brothers and sisters was that at least one of them was usually within earshot. Sure enough, this time it was Jake and Jeremy to the rescue. Jake later became a high-jumper in high school and Jeremy became a basketball player, so their skills at jumping were already budding. We had barbed wire fences stretched about four feet off the ground. Jake and Jeremy easily cleared them by two feet, arrived with dispatch, and pulled the rebellious fence off me.

As for Polly, as soon as she heard me bellowing like a fool calf, she hightailed it out of the country. She wasn't about to be blamed for my mishap. Her fleeing fanny was the last thing I saw as I was being wrestled to the ground.

However, this was not my only encounter with electric fences. One of the most exciting games that we played as youngsters was a game called "Ghost in the Graveyard." This game required one of us to put our hands over our eyes and lean up against a tree or wall of the house or any other thing we called "base." As the rest of the kids went to hide, the person at the tree cried out, "One o'clock, two o'clock, three o'clock," and so on until he or she reached twelve o'clock. At that point, the person would yell, "Ghost in the graveyard!" He or she would then have to go look for all the people who were hiding, while they, in the meantime, would try to leave their hiding places without being detected and run back to the base. This was all done in practically pitch- black darkness.

It was during one of these games that I was jumped by an electric fence. At that time, we had a double-wire electric fence holding goats in one section of the pasture. All our other electric fences were only one strand, and we had gotten very adept at ducking under these without missing a step. We were so familiar with the farm that we knew instinctively where the fences were and could navigate around them in near blackness. On this particular occasion, I was running with lightning speed as one of the kids was hollering out the countdown. I dropped down to my knees to crawl under the wire, lunged rapidly forward to skirt under the fence, when ka-wham! I was knocked flat on the ground. The electric fence had caught me right on the forehead. My whole head lit up inside like a psychedelic kaleidoscope. I saw concentric rings of color pulsating out from the center of a bright star. It was if I were inside a bursting firework in a Fourth of July display. I had no idea what had hit me and lay there stunned. As the effect of the electric shock dispelled from my overcharged brain, it began to dawn on me that I had forgotten that there were two strands of wire on this fence, and my crawling height was just the right height to connect with the bottom strand. Boy, was I a bit wobbly as I made it back to base. You'd think that those fences would have had enough of me, but they were just warming up.

Whack!

"What did you do that for?" I said as I stood rubbing the back of my head.

Jeremy and I were playing with our wooden boats in the cow trough, and I had just been hit on the back of the head. Or at least I thought I had been.

It just so happened that at that time, I had put all the "don'ts" concerning electricity into a file, sorted them, catalogued them, and, after having put them all in their places, rolled them all together into one big "DO":

Don't allow a highly conductive piece of metal, such as iron, to contact an electrical source.

Don't let water contact any electrical source.

Never be in water or stand in water when there is the possibility of electric shock.

Always have a piece of rubber or another non-conductive material between you and an electrified material before touching it.

Be sure there is an alternate path for the electrical current to the ground other than through your body.

All of these are perfectly sensible rules. But rules can't put sense into the rule-maker—and I hadn't made sure I was following the rules. I had a boat to float, and these rules were the farthest things from my mind—with the possible exception of the price of tea in China. As Jeremy and I had leaned over the cow trough with our hands submerged in the water, racing our boats around, the back of my head had touched the electrical wire. There were no light shows this time; I think all the synapses in my brain were already fried. I just felt as if I had been struck on the back of the head by a two-by-four.

The water trough for the cows was a large cast-iron claw-foot bathtub. Our hands were fully submerged in water. We were the only source for the electrical path, and my curly hair did not qualify as an insulator. In one fell swoop, I had broken all the rules on electricity. In general, when rules are broken, someone else also gets hurt. The charged water also electrocuted Jeremy, and he flew out of there as if he'd been shot out of one of the imaginary cannons on his boat. When our wits returned and we figured out what had happened, we started laughing and rolling on the ground, poking fun at each other as to who had looked the most ridiculous exploding out of the tub.

The electric fence had more than one way of catching us unawares. Zapping us one at a time was good; two at a time was better; and, as I am about to relate, when it nailed a whole passel of us kids with one shot, that was the best of all.

One summer evening, Jeremy's friend John from across the field came over at milking time with two of his friends from the city. One was another boy, and the other was his cute sister. They were all full of questions about how a cow was milked. First, we had to inform them that, no, pumping the tail was not always necessary. We only did that if the spigots were dry and the pump needed priming; otherwise we just followed the instructions. And, no, you did not get chocolate milk from brown cows. You had to feed them cocoa beans with their grain, as the powdered chocolate that they had in the city only made the cow sneeze and her eyes water. City folk were well-served to leave those kinds of details to professionals like us.

We had Pumpkin, a Guernsey cow, pleasantly munching her grain in the stanchion, and we commenced to show them how to milk. Jeremy was the natural instructor, as he was older—and he was also showing off to the cute little girl. Jeremy scooted his milk stool up close to the cow and reached under her, grabbing hold of the spigot closest to him. The little girl crouched Indian style next to him and grabbed the back spigot in her hand. Jeremy proceeded to explain how to properly squeeze the teat, so that milk would come out easily, with no discomfort to the cow.

By this time, the lesson was turning into a community event. Pumpkin looked around nervously, not liking how the event was unfolding: one cow, four teats, ten little hands, and nowhere to run. John was leaning on the little girl's back to see, and the girl's brother was leaning on Jeremy's shoulder. Impressing the city gal, I was propped against Pumpkin's shoulder as cool as a country boy. As the whole milking side of the cow was filled up, one youngster who was left out but who wanted to see the lesson whipped around to the other side of the cow where there were two free spigots. He reached in eagerly, grasped the cow's teat with his hand, and POW! all mayhem broke loose. As the cow's rear end collapsed, kids were flung in all directions, arms and legs flailing. We scrambled to our feet and gingerly rubbed ourselves, watching the cow heave herself back on her hooves.

We all looked around at each other in dazed amazement, wondering what on Earth had hit us. A little detective work revealed that the youngster, while reaching in, had touched his head on the electric fence that ran along the side of the milking stanchion, electrocuting us all. Electric fences were always waylaying us and giving us a jolt whenever they could catch us off guard.

EVERY HAIR COUNTED

We were commiserating over haircuts. Yep, we were definitely the most miserable bunch of miserators that ever gathered to misorate. Dad's haircutting shears had once again found our heads and reduced them to bare fields of short stubble. This semiannual ritual of haircutting always seemed to fall at the most inconvenient times. We hated to get haircuts even at the best of times. This was the sixties, and short hair—especially militarily short hair—was definitely not in. We were eating well, taking our vitamins, and getting plenty of rest so we could come up with a really respectable crop of hair. At the age of eleven or twelve, we were just coming to an age when girls might (by some stretch of our imaginations) look at us. Don Juan was nearing retirement, and we boys thought we had a fighting chance to replace him.

Dad had other ideas, however, and we would find ourselves in an ever-expanding group out in the woods waiting for the next victim of Dad's knife to arrive so that we could examine the damage. At first, a sad face of condolence would greet the new arrival. Then, when all of us had been fleeced, there would be statements to buck up our courage in the face of obvious defeat. We would offer statements like, "It doesn't look that bad," or "It'll grow back fast," or "It doesn't look that bad from the back." We all knew these were said to apply balm to the anguished soul, as sorrow shared is sorrow lessened, but the words could not extinguish the cold, hard fact: *we were bald*.

On the other hand, an amazing thing resulted from this gloomy gathering—a firestorm of humor, the effects of which we carry to this day. It would start with feeble attempts to cajole good nature out of a grieving boy. We would start comparing his looks to some kind of natural phenomenon or freak of nature. By doing this, we were able to provoke laughter, and soon we would all be sharing knee-slappingly funny jokes. This is how we came up with nicknames for each other that have stuck with us to this day.

After one exceptionally egregious attack on our mops, just one day before a school picnic and two days before the end of the school year, we found ourselves standing around the woods in the depths of despondency when suddenly the power of regeneration kicked in and our fertile minds began to think of funny names. It started with a few names that were only starters and had no lasting power, but as we got warmed up, we became more inventive. Following the logic of simple association, inference, and the characteristics or qualities existing in each boy, we ended up with our permanent appellations.

Jeremy, being the oldest participant at that time, and being the most muscular and athletic, was named Chief Little Muscles. (If memory serves me right, Ivan came up with that one.) I, the next in age but the skinniest of the bunch, was christened Plump Woman. (I took some umbrage at that, as I was not plump.) Again, I think Ivan came up with that one. Ivan himself was next to be fingered, and we saddled him with Sergeant Skinhead. Peter, who was of a bit rounder stature at that age and whose head we thought resembled Charlie Brown, wound up as President Blockhead. Tristan stepped in line to become Colonel Stringbean. And, last but not least, Damien was pinned with Captain Floodpants, due to the hand-me-down nature of the pants he was wearing. (They could be kept safely dry in a flood with water as high as his Adam's apple.)

The next year, we found ourselves in the very same situation, and the creative juices were flowing once more. There were two mountains about seventy miles north of our home, and Jake, Jeremy, and I hiked from one to the other one summer. The two mountains were called North and South Baldy, with North Baldy being much more pointed at the top while South Baldy was more rounded. Both mountains were covered by high meadows except at their peaks, hence their names. Father Time had bestowed on them the same affliction we suffered from: baldness. To this day, I am North Baldy and Ivan is South Baldy.

We tried the same tactics that the mountains did to hide their shame. They covered their heads with snow and tried to pull their tree lines up their sloping shoulders. We tried on as many hats as we could, hiked our shirt or coat collars as high as we could, and asked each other, "How does this look?"

The answer would always be, "Oh, sure, the girls will hardly notice a thick stocking hat and parka in the middle of the summer," or, "Do you think my girlfriend would notice if I wore this white sailor's hat with the brim turned down?" (We called them our "girlfriends" even if they didn't know we existed—especially this one girl I had a crush on that lasted longer than most marriages today). This crush lasted from about third grade until we left eighth grade. No, this wasn't the first girlfriend I'd ever had. There was a little cutie that I used to escort around the halls in second grade. I know second grade was a little late to start looking for a spouse, but with all the farm responsibilities that I had, I only had so much free time. That romance lasted until I asked her if I could hold her hand on the way to music class. She said "No." Gosh, I thought, what does this girl want? I knew I could provide it.

I could shoot squirrels with my slingshot, jump up and down on my right leg twenty times without even touching my left to the ground, and I could tie both shoes without looking. I planned to grow muscles soon and could recite every word to the ditty, *"Way down south where the bananas grow, a grasshopper stepped on an elephant's toe. The elephant said with tears in his eyes, 'Go pick on someone your own size.'"* She must have lacked the judgment of a more mature woman. I was, after all, two months older, and I probably scared her with all my accomplishments.

But back to haircuts. After we had been scalped one Saturday, we had to attend church the next day. Our family was already a subject of discussion on account of all the children we had, and this Sunday was no exception. We found ourselves in the front row, all lined up according to age, Jake being the oldest still living at home. Of course, we all felt as if every eye was turned on us and our newly shaved heads. This humiliation was bad enough. But after we thought that perhaps we were not being scrutinized and might be able to slink from Mass undetected, the scripture of the day was delivered: "For know that every hair on your head is counted." Of all the Sundays of the year, of all the scripture passages there are, how could *that* be the one for the day?

All of our faces, and of course the backs of our heads, turned bright red, as surely every eye in the congregation must have been directed at us. I don't remember who couldn't repress their giggle, but every one of us—Jake, Jeremy, yours truly, Ivan, Peter,

Tristan, and Damien—was trying to choke back our laughter. The whole pew was shaking. Occasionally, a squeak would escape under intense pressure, usually from Jeremy, right when the rest of us had managed a bit of composure, and then off we would go again in paroxysms of laughter, just barely suppressed to maintain the solemnity of Holy Mass. All we prayed for that day was a miracle drug for hair growth. We prayed that it would be put on the market the very next day—and that we would be the first in line to buy it!

MARVIN THE MAGPIE

"Can you see?"

"Almost, just a little more," I said as I stretched myself full-length to get a glimpse into the magpie nest. Sure enough, the egg still rested there, unharmed. Backing down from this perch fifteen feet off the water was a real challenge. The alder tree I was in slanted over an overgrown beaver pond about two miles the way the crow flies north of our house.

There were three main routes that we could take to the Big Stream (as we called the place). One way was to head straight north up the quarter-mile driveway, across the county road, through a barbed wire fence, and then through woods and meadow until arriving at the Big Stream.

Another way was to head west on the county road. At that time it was a small lane that took us up to the southern slope of the Big Hill. Here we would strike north, following a field up the side of the hill until we reached the woods. Then we would head to the west, up over the top of the Big Hill, around the big boulders, and then straight north through the woods, past the springs, and on to the Big Stream.

The third way was to continue west up the county road until it ran into a fence at the woods. We would continue through the fence until we skirted around the Big Hill entirely, past the homestead of some forgotten pioneer, and past a small creek down the side of a small ridgeback packed with beautiful alders and other creek bed flora, until we reached the Little Stream. By following the Little Stream downstream, we would be led to the Big Stream. Every route had its own peculiar character and beauty and, hence, provided us with many different adventures as we traversed the woods, meadows, and streams. Sometimes we were the hunter, sometimes the explorer, and sometimes just the fascinated observer of nature at work.

Ivan and I made this two-mile hike three or four more times before we were finally rewarded with the first sight of a baby magpie. We were then able to watch its growth over the next couple of trips back to the Big Stream. I was eleven and he was nine, and I had determined, after having no luck with wounded baby songbirds, that a bird had no chance of survival until it was fully feathered. I determined that this was when a bird's stomach became less sensitive to a change of diet.

The day had finally arrived to capture this little bird and make him my pet. I climbed gingerly up the slanted alder, both to keep from tumbling into the water and to avoid scaring him out of his nest. I carefully extended my hand until it was even with the bottom of the nest and raised my head slowly to peer over the side. To my dismay and discomfiture, there was nothing left but a few feathers. Some predator must have gotten there first. Sure enough, after exploring the mud around the base of the tree, we discovered raccoon tracks. I was devastated. I had only discovered this one nest, and that was the last chance I had that year. But the following year yielded better results.

Armed with a fuller knowledge of magpies, we set about our quest for a nest in the cackleberry bushes lining the Big Stream. Well I *thought* they were cackle-berry bushes. Only much later in life I learned that cackleberries are *hen's* eggs. The magpies didn't seem to mind my error; they nested there just the same. I had learned that magpies seldom nested anywhere other than in the densest and thorniest bushes they could find. Not only did they nest in these places; they would build a canopy of thorny twigs over their nests, with one hole to go in and another to depart, because they had no way of turning around on account of their long tails.

We scoured the bushes and trees until we spotted a nest high off the ground. The nest was ten to twenty feet off the ground and posed a real challenge. Not only were the branches of the tree covered with inch-long needlepoint thorns; the trunks were, too. It was only with gingerly movements that I could navigate up the unfriendly beast. And the trunk did not have regular branches sticking out of its sides to help the steps of a vertical traveler. No, I had to press my shoe against the trunk and lunge to catch a hold higher up. If I was lucky enough not to impale my hand or stick a thorn through my shoe, I would then grab even higher up with my other hand.

After I had popped my head up into the canopy of thorny branches (and been stabbed on the top of my head with a woodpecker-like thorn), I explored with my other foot for a foothold. As I did this, the tree was plotting its next move. When I pushed to propel myself higher up into the tree, it wrapped a thorny tendril around my arm and held on tight. This was at the same time that my foot let loose. Instead of my free hand grabbing a strategically located place on the branches higher up, it was forced to grab wherever it could.

Grab it did, and steadfastly too—unfortunately, it was impaled by the biggest and nastiest thorn on the whole tree! I couldn't release my grip, so I had to go up higher as soon as my lower limbs and my other arm found a hold. By this point, I was bleeding, hot, and sweaty, and there was still that nest to examine. With painstaking care, I slowly bent back the thorny branches and hooked them around other branches to move them out of my way.

By doing this, I basically guaranteed a swift kick in the rear from four or five angry thorns as the branch let go and smacked me with a vengeance.

At this point, both my posterior and anterior were a mess of scratches and punctures. But the thrill of the hunt had begun, and this tree was destined to be conquered. The prize? To get a good look in that nest to see if it held any young feathered friends.

Alas, it did not!

Now I had to navigate back down the tree without adding to my wounds. As I stood there catching my breath for a moment, blood trickled down my neck and face from my various cuts. I asked Ivan if he saw any more nests. First, he asked me if I was all right, fulfilling the role of the concerned brother, but really he was just as keen as I was to get on to the next one. I replied that it was only a scratch, and we plunged eagerly into the thicket in search of a new nest.

Later in the afternoon, Ivan and I were scouring the creek bottom for a nest when we heard a cacophony of a whole flock of magpies making their way catty-corner across an alfalfa field. We ran out of the thicket and saw that some of the birds were youngsters. We could tell they were not long out of the nest because their tails were very short. Their inability to keep up with the flock whetted our appetite, and the chase was on!

What would last longer: their young wings or our young legs? It was hard to tell because we had to wear them out before they could reach the woods on the other side of the field. They were about twenty yards ahead of us and fifty or so feet in the air, squawking like the dickens as we chased them, leaving a trail of dust in our wake. Our lungs began to ache and our tongues began to get tripped up in our legs when we noticed that the babies were losing altitude fast and might not make it to the woods. We poured on the coal and closed the gap. Just short of a huge ponderosa pine, one of them fell to the ground in exhaustion, and we captured him as he scrambled to escape.

What a happy ending!

I wrapped him up in my T-shirt, and we started for home, chattering about the excitement of the chase and all the cool things I would be able to do with the bird. I named that first magpie Pirate, a name which ended up being far too appropriate—because he ended up being untamable. I spent two weeks trying to coax him to come to me. But he always remained out of reach—no matter how long I stood with food in my hand. He would look at it quizzically, and go round and around his cage to look at it from every angle, muttering and chattering to himself—but he would never give in.

After two weeks of this, I came up with a brilliant idea. I would tie a string to his leg and let him out, much like a kite. Then I could at least do something with him, and maybe over time he would get used to me. Nothing doing! He would just spend his whole time pecking and pecking at that blasted thing on his leg—until I would be worn out with frustration and disappointment. Dejectedly, I would return him to the cage.

In the end, his stubbornness was his own undoing. Even after Cecilia and I had gone way out in a grassy meadow and caught him half a jar-full of big, fat grasshoppers, he refused to eat. I even left him a whole ground squirrel that I had shot with an arrow, and he still refused, thumbing his nose in defiance. No matter what I offered, he refused it, until at last he died of starvation.

The next year, I went out to the Big Stream again. But this time I was convinced that I had to get a fully feathered bird, not yet out of the nest. Back up into the cackleberry bushes I went. Wounded and bleeding, I went from nest to nest, looking for the perfect magpie fortress to storm. One day in early May, I was finally able to capture a young magpie, just ready to leave the nest. I wrapped him gingerly in my shirt and marched him home where I had devised a better method to tame him and make him my friend. I placed him in a pen I had put together from an old rabbit cage. It stood on stilts, so I could easily reach in, and I blocked off part of it so that he could never be entirely out of my reach.

A young bird like the one I had caught needs to eat about once an hour. Every time I went out to feed him, I would call his name and whistle. This, of course, was to train him by stimuli and response, like Pavlov's dogs, only without the slobber. I would reach in and corner him as he tried to elude my grasp. When I caught him, I would wrap my whole hand around him, thereby pinning his wings down but leaving his feet free. I would then bring a grasshopper up close to his mouth, and when he struggled and opened his mouth to bite me, I quickly shoved the grasshopper into his mouth and down his gullet. It only took a few feedings for him to figure out that I was his food supply. He no longer needed to be caught but would crouch with his wings quivering, squawking and crying like a baby, snapping his mouth wide open when a grasshopper appeared. This was when I knew that I had removed his fear of his new surroundings.

The next step was to get him to voluntarily step up on to the finger of my left hand as I held a grasshopper in my right. This posed a new challenge to him, another fear for him to overcome. The greatest obstacle for him was my inability to keep from laughing at his histrionics as he tried to get to the grasshopper without touching my out-stretched finger. He would complain with the most pitiful noises, squawking and hollering his indignation, all the while stretching out his neck as far as he could until he looked more like a goose than a magpie. Eventually, he would give up in frustration, hopping around the cage in a huff until hunger overcame him again. Then he would swallow his pride and fight another round.

Lots of patience was required to play this game, and I would stand there like a statue for half an hour or more, trying not to twitch a muscle. At last, he would lift his foot, place it on my finger, and lunge for the food I gave him as a reward for his valiant leap of faith. After only a few more grasshoppers, he learned that a full stomach was well worth the risk. Soon he learned to leap with alacrity onto my finger. He perched there until he was stuffed so full that he could only whimper, his pipes having been so pressed in by gluttony that little air could be forced past.

Because I always preceded his feedings by whistling and calling his name, he quickly learned to anticipate dinner, and he would respond with cries of impatience as I approached his cage. Immediately, he would jump on my fingers and perch there until he was satisfied. It only took about four days to get him to this stage. First, he would satisfy his hunger; *then* he would satisfy his curiosity. And *that* was when the real fun began.

His curiosity would be fully engaged when examining my arm all the way to my hand. With his head cocked slightly to one side, he would examine my skin and then—WHIP!—he would peck whatever imperfection caught his eye. Cuts, bruises, elbow bones, or anything else that seemed odd was fair game. His examination was both charming and painful; and more than once he was toppled from his perch as I flinched in indignation and knocked him backwards.

The next step in his education was to introduce him to the world outside his cage. I would leave the cage door open, stand about a foot from the entrance, and bend my arm at the elbow with my index finger extended. Then I would hold a grasshopper with my right hand about two inches from my index finger and shake it, all the while whistling and calling his name. He would run back and forth across the edge of the open cage, stop, look down over the edge, look back up, and gauge the distance to my hand. Finally, hunger demanded action, and he would squawk and leap on to my finger. Over time, I drew him out farther and farther, until he had to fly to get to my hand.

You might be wondering how I got all those grasshoppers to feed the bird's prodigious appetite. I spent so much time with grasshoppers that summer that hopping, skipping, and jumping became my natural mode of travel. It was fortuitous that this year of the magpie coincided with the point in our seasonal cycle when we had hordes of grasshoppers.

There were three methods that I used to catch these critters. One was the obvious method. I would crouch down, lean forward, lunge, and slap the ground with my hand. However, this method was tedious, as I could only capture one or two of them at a time. The hoppers were usually wary, and I often came up empty- handed.

The next method I came up with was to use a whip. I cut three long strips of black rubber from an old car inner tube. These strips were about three feet long and an inch wide. I nailed them to a handle fashioned from a tree branch, and then I had a whip that would have made any sea captain proud. With this whip, I would march out into the yard, spot three or more grasshoppers on the ground, and CRACK! I would bring the whip down and flog the bunch of them. This was much more efficient than my original method, and I used this technique with gusto.

However, I noticed that there were sometimes concentrations of twenty-five or more grasshoppers per square foot. I knew I could increase my yield eight times over if I could find a way to capture all of them at once. A piece of screen from an old screen door provided me with just the tool that I needed. I cut out a two-square-foot section of screen before throwing it across the yard like a Frisbee. I would run over and pin it down, slowly raising the screen and removing the grasshoppers one at a time until I had gathered the whole lot. Other members of the family couldn't help but observe this action as I provided food for my adopted friend. (My manner of crazed running combined with my drumstick-legs—about the same size as my bird's—earned me the name of Banty Legs from one of my brothers-in-law.)

Meanwhile, my bird training continued. A few days of having Marvin (as I had come to call the magpie) fly onto my hand emboldened him, and his confidence grew. He especially liked to land on my head, as he could get a good grip on my mop of curly hair. Although *he* enjoyed this advantage, *I* didn't. His needle-like claws tended to dig into my scalp. When he reached this level of confidence, he rode around on my finger, and as I bent down to grab a grasshopper, he scrambled around to my back and perched there awaiting his dinner.

While he rode around on me, Ivan, Cecilia, Peter,

Tristan, and Damien would all assume various positions on the ground as they caught grasshoppers. When one of them was successful, they would stand up, hold the grasshopper pinned between a finger and thumb, and wiggle it, while at the same time whistling to get Marvin's attention. When Marvin saw this, he would fly over, land on the outstretched arm, and then peck the grasshoppers from the person's fingers. In this way, he would go from one to the other, until he was so stuffed he'd have to quit and rest.

Marvin's habit of landing on my head began to carry over onto other unsuspecting victims. At one point, our cousins from California were visiting for a week. They had four little kids, one of whom was a two-year-old named Charlie. He was walking from the house to their car, when suddenly we heard a terrified scream. When we got to him, we found Marvin trying feverishly to get a grip on little Charlie's head, as the toddler ducked and screamed and ran terrified toward the house.

A similar situation arose when Mrs. Miller, a neighbor with a bouffant hairdo, went out to hang her wash one morning. Out of nowhere, Marvin descended from on high, landing on her puffed up coiffeur. I don't know who was more surprised, Mrs. Miller for having her noggin attacked and her sixty dollar bouffant exploded, or Marvin, who was expecting a friendly perch, with breakfast and a little gossip, before starting his day. Needless to say, Mrs. Miller was not pleased.

My little sister Jessica—who was barely one but

was walking and talking—would cover her head and duck down any time Marvin came near her. But it was amazing how even she became attached to the bird, as was evident one day when Lee, a friend of my brother, came down to visit in his pickup. As he began to drive away after his visit, Jessica started crying and frantically waving. She was trying to say that Lee was taking the bird, and, sure enough, Marvin was perched on the side mirror, enjoying the ride. Lee stopped and returned the hitchhiker, and Jessica was mollified.

My little pet afforded me hours of entertainment and pleasure. We could spend half an hour just playing catch-his-beak. I would place my thumb, index finger, and next finger together at the tips to form a triangular hole. I would then move them in and out and Marvin would peck in the hole. By pinching my fingers together I could grab his beak and he would be stuck. Thus captured, he would plant his feet firmly and pull with all his might, all the while shaking his head vigorously from side to side. Right when he would be pulling his hardest, I would release my fingers and he would fall over backwards, wings flapping as he tried to keep his balance. But he would always pop right up and start pecking again and again until I caught him—and I would feel his wrath if I didn't catch him. Magpies have a very strong beak made for ripping apart carrion and other highly desirable foodstuffs. Man, oh man, could he peck hard on my fingers if I didn't pay attention!

Another of his and my favorite games was for him to pull my handkerchief out of my front pocket.

I would sit on the ground playing with him, leaving just a tiny speck of the handkerchief showing. Then Marvin would sidle up, look things over, hop up onto my leg, and get a grip on that corner. He would shake his whole body back and forth as he tugged and tugged to get that handkerchief out. It would slowly inch out, and—right at the last moment—it would let loose and Marvin would go tumbling. As soon as Marvin got it out, he would expect me to put it right back in my pocket. If I didn't, he would stand there with it stuffed in his mouth, trying to squawk his insistence and sounding like a sick crow. Then he would peck at my leg by the pocket, and I would dutifully please my friend and start the game over again.

Marvin enjoyed this game so much that if I slept outside over-night, at the crack of dawn he would begin to peck me as I lay under my blankets. He allowed for no laziness and barked out his orders like any good drill sergeant. He would try to pull off my covers or otherwise bruise me up with that powerful beak, so that I had no choice but to come out from under the covers.

During that summer, Leo had gotten into the habit of sleeping outside. He worked for the local farmers, cutting and bucking hay and driving a combine during the wheat harvest. After my magpie learned that there was somebody under the mounds of material, he was fair game in Marvin's opinion. And he was opinionated! He shared his opinions loudly in the early dawn hours to anyone who cared (or didn't care) to listen. His opinions, however, were met with much annoyance by anyone still trying to get some sleep. The family voted unanimously that the Bill of Rights and freedom of speech did not apply to bird-brains, and that, therefore, the law could not prevent anyone from taking matters into his or her own hands. The magpie opined that since he had a *bill*, those rights *did* apply to him—and he continued his harangues.

That summer, Leo purchased a sleeping bag that could be seen from Mars because it was so bright orange. If no one else was sleeping outside that night, Marvin would assume that Leo would take over the responsibility of entertaining him in the morning. First, he ascertained if there were any parts of the human anatomy left exposed. In Leo's case, this wasn't possible, as his new sleeping bag was one of those newfangled mummy bags that engulfed the occupant like a cocoon. Now, this posed a challenge to Marvin. He would perch on the highest part of the sleeping bag and WHAM, WHAM, WHAM—there would be no response. WHAM, WHAM, WHAM. Now there would be a stirring WHAM, WHAM, WHAM, even harder. By this point, he would usually have Leo's attention. Leo would poke his head out while sputtering from the depths of sleep "What in darnation is that?" His thrashing about would result in Marvin's temporary retreat to gauge how much danger he might be in. After Leo would retract his head like an insulted turtle, Marvin would fly to the top of the mountain and begin his mining again. It would only take a few more of these episodes to fully exasperate Leo, and he would have to retreat into the house if he wanted to get any more sleep.

After a couple of days of this, Marvin figured out that his fun would be spoiled if he pestered too insistently. But then he discovered a most peculiar phenomenon. By pecking on the seam line of the sleeping bag, he could get a thread to loosen up. If Marvin got hold of a little thread and did some gentle tugging, he would begin to reveal the innermost entrails of the bag. With a little patience, he could coax out some pure- white Dacron 88. This could have contributed to a whole summer of fun for Marvin. Unfortunately for him, his delights did not have quite the same effect on Leo. When Leo thrust his head out and discovered this egregious attack on his person and possessions, he had had enough and he told Mom that the bird had to go. Well, go he did, but in the most unexpected of ways.

In those days, I used to sleep outside with a blanket. When Marvin played with me, I didn't mind because he was my friend. On one occasion, it was a good thing he was my friend, because it was the only thing that kept me from ringing his little neck. We had this little game going where he would look for me under the covers. I would lie stretched out on the ground and lift the edge of the blanket just enough so that, by crouching on the ground and peering under, Marvin could see me there. Then I would lift the blanket a little more, and, just as he got his head under it, I would clamp it down on his head. He would squawk in protest and scramble away. But Marvin loved this game, and he would come right back looking for me under the covers. One of these times, I was teasing him especially well. I had the blanket about an inch above the ground with my eyes peering out, watching him pace back and forth about four inches away, with his head right next to the ground. In the intensity of watching him and laughing at his discomfiture, I inadvertently placed my eyes up close to the opening. Marvin must have seen the glitter of my eye, because with lightning speed, he pecked me right in the eye before I had a chance to blink.

I popped up so fast that weasels would have been wowed at the speed. I grabbed my eye in pain and checked to make sure it was still in the socket. When I had made sure that my eye was intact, I had to determine if Marvin's should stay that way as well. Luckily for him, the bonds of friendship held fast and melted my anger into laughter. And, of course, there were many more occasions for laughter.

At that time, we had a lab-pointer mix named Sam. He was a wonderful family pet. He would chase birds across the forty acre field for the pure pleasure of it and obligingly eat rocks out of the hands of the baby siblings (while thumbing his nose at adults who tried to do the same). He was taught to retrieve anything that was thrown for him. More often than not, it would be a pine cone he had found in the woods, and, after much sport with it, the pine cone would turn into a slobbery piece of work. He would bring it up to anyone who seemed lively enough to throw, looked expectantly at their faces, and begged them to throw it.

Occasionally, we would see the dog chasing Marvin, with the magpie screaming in fear—or so it seemed. One day, we were all sitting down to a two-hundred-pound pot of spaghetti when we heard the all-too-familiar sound of the dog barking and the bird squawking. I ran to the window to scold Sam, but to my dismay, it was not the dog who was at fault, but Marvin. The dog was running and ducking across the front yard as Marvin nose-dived him from the air. They were both enjoying the sport, and Mom said no more scolding the dog. If the bird got it, then he deserved it. But Sam tired of the chase as soon as he finally determined he would never enjoy the fruits of his labor for dinner. After that, he just ignored Marvin's provocations. But this didn't sit well with Marvin, so he devised other ways to get the dog's attention.

The slimy pine cone Sam would beg us to throw became the next tool Marvin used to annoy the dog. When Sam would look for someone to throw the pine cone, Marvin would land on the ground about five feet away. He would crouch down and begin to sidle up to it, taking a few cautionary hops toward Sam to see if the dog had noticed him. Then he would take a few more steps, this time a little closer. Sam would see him from the corner of his eye and lunge at the bird, and Marvin would just barely elude the jaws and fly to a perch where he could scream and scold Sam, as if Marvin was the one being assaulted. After that, he would hop right back down to start it all over again. But Sam soon tired of this as well and ignored Marvin—until Marvin got braver.

When Rossini wrote his opera *The Thieving Magpie*, he must have recalled a thieving magpie in action. The music is a perfect imitation of magpie thievery. When Sam had a pine cone, Marvin would make his advance—a little closer, a little closer, and a little closer. Just a few more hops, and he would be right under the dog 's mouth. He would stretch his neck out, grab the pine cone firmly, and drag it right out from under Sam. This was too much even for Sam, and he would go after Marvin. At those times Marvin seemed to have a rubber band connecting him to Sam. As soon as he was out of range of Sam's jaws, he would go right back to teasing him again—much to our delight and Sam's chagrin.

Sam eventually figured out that he was the loser, and he would let the magpie drag the pine cone away.

Well, this was no fun for Marvin. He needed the excitement of the chase. So, what was he to do? His only recourse was to inflict pain. Again, since this was a new assault and demanded great caution, he would follow the score of *The Thieving Magpie* and begin his antics. This time, he would assault the dog from the rear. Working his way forward to Sam's back foot while the dog was begging, he grabbed a chunk of Sam's hair and began tugging. Sam's patience would give way to anger, and he would head after the bird. This worked again and again, much to Marvin's delight, until, Sam would again resign himself to the torment.

But Marvin wasn't finished. The next step was to sneak up and peck at Sam's foot, HARD. I knew the power of that beak and how much it hurt. After a few chases, Sam eventually overcame even this provocation and would just quit and go find something else to do away from the bird.

The affection I felt for my pet magpie was not shared equally by my siblings. Of course, the level of affection varied as their experiences with Marvin's antics grew. Mom, whose patience knew no bounds, was sorely tested when Marvin invited himself into the house and helped himself to a couple of big beak-fulls of butter sitting out on the kitchen table. Or when he would start going through the shiny objects on Mom's dresser to see which one he might be able to steal. Leaving the back door open was always an invitation to Marvin to make himself at home.

All of this fun and excitement came to an end one day, as Marvin's curiosity led him farther and farther away from home.

I never needed to put him in his cage, because after about two weeks he would just hole up for the night under the leaves of our plum tree. But, one day, I came home from ground-squirrel hunting with my bow and arrow and missed his noisy welcome. He had flown to the wild blue yonder.

The problem was I couldn't fly into the wild blue yonder, so I lost my feathered friends—but not before they had filled my summer days with happiness.

ADIEU

It's time for me to go now.

The crickets are quieting down.

Just a few last plaintive chirrups and then to bed.

You have helped me chase Alone away from Grandma for a while—and what a pleasure it's been to re-live my adventures with you!

Alone will sneak back into Grandma's place after we go—so you will have to come back with me to chase him away.

There are so many more adventures to be told.

CPSIA information can be obtained
at www.ICGtesting.com
Printed in the USA
BVHW030727290719
554557BV00001B/134/P